Missing Under The Mistletoe

A Flower Shop Mystery
Christmas Novella

Kate Collins

MISSING UNDER THE MISTLETOE
A Flower Shop Mystery Christmas Novella

ISBN: 9781983147197

Cover design by Arash Jahani

CONTENTS

'Twas the day before Christmas
 on New Chapel square
Not a storefront was empty,
not a street corner bare
The red and green lights on the trees
were a glowing,
And last-minute shoppers held bags
overflowing
For in a few hours the bells
would be rung;
The tree would be lit,
and the carols all sung

But there were a few who were
not in the spirit,
While mysteries beckoned
all those who would hear it
For even through trouble,
though heartaches evolve,
There were gifts to deliver
and cases to solve
And Bloomers was nestled
in one prime location,
to bask in the town's
Christmas Eve celebration.

CHAPTER ONE

Bloomers Flower Shop
December 24th
9:30 am

"Abby," I heard Lottie call, trying her best to maintain a cheerful tone, "could you come out here for a minute? We have customers waiting."

I poked my head through the purple curtain separating the workroom from the sales floor and saw that Bloomers was already packed. Giving me a pointed, impatient stare was Mrs. Guilford, standing in front of the register holding a long branch of mistletoe, her wallet out, with one white glove pushed back just far enough to check her gold and diamond-laced wristwatch.

Meanwhile, Lottie, my long-time assistant, was bouncing between two couples with her hands full. Literally. She had a potted poinsettia in one hand and a white lily gift basket in the other. I immediately stopped what I was doing and headed for the register.

Normally I enjoyed the Christmas Eve morning rush, but the spindle in the workroom was still half-full of orders that needed to be finished before the store closed at four o'clock, Lottie was besieged by customers needing help in selecting gifts, Grace was attending to thirsty customers in the coffee-and-tea parlor, and Rosa hadn't yet returned from an early morning delivery. That left me popping back and forth between the workroom and shop floor trying to be everywhere at once. My head was spinning.

As I passed the parlor, I paused at the wide, arched doorway to ask Grace if she had a moment to spare, but she lifted her hands to show me a silver teapot and a plate of piping hot scones on their way to be delivered. "I wish I had time to help you out, love, but as you can see, we're jammed."

Scones. My mouth watered at the sight of Grace's homemade scones, today's flavor -blueberry pecan. I knew I should have had Rosa make her famous egg dish, *huevos ranchero,* before sending her out for that delivery. I'd hurried out of the house without having a bite since the shops around the square opened early on the morning before Christmas. Now I was starving, as I was sure my employees were. But the holidays were always crazy at Bloomers Flower Shop, so I just had to suck it up.

Where was I? Oh, yeah. *Breakfast.*

"Excuse me, Ms. Knight, but would you hurry, please?" Mrs. Guilford asked. "I am a very busy woman."

Oh, right. Mrs. Guilford.

I pushed a lock of my bright red hair out of my eyes. I'd barely had time to blow it into its usual long bob that morning and one side was hanging in my eyes and driving me crazy. "It's Abby Knight *Salvare,* now. And of course, I'll hurry. I'm so sorry you had to wait."

Rosa suddenly burst into Bloomers accompanied by a blast of cold air, causing the jingle bells we'd hung above the door to unharmoniously crash into the ceiling, stopping the store's bustle momentarily. Before scurrying past, she caught my eye, nodding her head toward the backroom, flailing the curtain behind her, leaving me standing awkwardly before my perplexed customer.

"I don't have time for this." And with that, Mrs. Guilford placed a twenty-dollar bill onto the counter. Picking up her mistletoe, she added, "Keep the change," then exited the shop in a rush.

Lottie, who had returned to the register to ring up one of her customers, leaned close to whisper, "Actually, the mistletoe was twenty-*one* dollars."

As I headed toward the workroom I thought back to earlier that morning when Grace, Rosa, Lottie, and I had taken a brisk, enchanting stroll around New Chapel's town square. We'd left just as the sun was peeking above the two and three-story nineteenth-century buildings, to catch a glimpse of the Christmas Eve preparations already underway.

From Bloomers, we'd taken the long way around the courthouse lawn, where booths were being constructed for vendors selling leftover holiday decorations, ornaments, knit-wear, snacks, and hot apple cider later that evening. On the other side of the courthouse stood Churchill's department store, the main Christmas shopping destination of downtown New Chapel, Indiana. The large, beautifully decorated old building occupied half a city block and was central to the annual Christmas Eve celebration.

After making a full circle around the square, we stopped to inspect our booth, just across the street from Bloomers, where we'd be selling arrangements of holly, mistletoe, and poinsettias. And that reminded me – I had to stop day-dreaming and get moving. Bloomers had been hired by Churchill's to deliver and display two dozen poinsettias before the store opened at ten o'clock that morning. I glanced at my watch. We only had twenty minutes.

When I entered the workroom, I found Rosa pacing back and forth, muttering something in Spanish as she fixed the black and gold headwrap that covered her ears. Poor Rosa.

It was her first year working for Bloomers and she wasn't accustomed to the holiday hassles.

"Rosa, you've got to chill out and tell me what's wrong."

"First, I am more than chilled. I am frozen stiff. I spent the last half hour standing on a small stool, hanging holly from the eaves of a Spanish colonial house, taking orders from a woman who seemed to think I knew only two words of English. *Here…*and *there!*

"And second, we have two dozen poinsettias and stands that still have to be delivered, carried inside, and arranged at Santa's Village before ten. How will we finish it all?*"

"It's okay, Rosa. We can be a little late."

"Ha! I used to work for Mr. Churchill and I will tell you this, he might look like *San Nicolás* but he is no saint. He does not tolerate his employees being late. Now, where are the poinsettias so I can start loading them? I have the delivery van waiting in the alley."

"You can't load them until the stands are inside the van. I'll have to give you a hand, though, because they're heavy."

"You do not have time for that and everyone else is too busy." She started for the cooler only to pause and glance back at me, one eyebrow cocked. "Unless you want to call Marco for help, as I suggested earlier."

"We don't need Marco." Which wasn't the truth, because the stands we used were made of heavy wrought iron so they wouldn't be easily tipped over by children waiting to see Santa. But I couldn't tell Rosa that because Marco and I hadn't parted on the best of terms that morning. "Grace and Lottie will just have to manage without me for a while."

I was about to follow Rosa to the cooler when a small Christmas miracle happened. I couldn't believe I was using those words to describe my zany cousin, but when the purple curtain parted, there stood the tall, beautiful Jillian Knight

Osborne with a teacup in hand, dressed almost head to toe in white.

She had on a white snow cap over her long copper-colored hair, a white turtle-neck sweater beneath a furry white vest, sparkly silver leggings, and bright white snow boots that looked like they had never even seen the snow.

Her smile turned to surprise as I rushed to hug her. "Jillian, thank God you're here! I need you out on the sales floor now."

She blinked back a sudden rush of tears. "You actually want my help?"

"Yes, so yank off that vest, grab one of the yellow smocks hanging in the storage closet, and get behind the register. That'll give Lottie a chance to catch up back here. You'll be fine."

She began listing off the reasons why she wouldn't be fine as I made my way back to the workroom. Rosa was inside one of our walk-in coolers, straining as she tried to drag two of the heavy wrought iron stands through the door.

"Rosa, you're going to hurt your back. We'll have to lift them together. Maybe take one out at a time."

"Twenty-four stands and then twenty-four poinsettias one by one? I'm telling you, Abby, we need Marco's help."

"No, we don't. We can do this if we work together." The heavy stand was stacked on top of another. We lifted them together toward the back door, then stopped. My arms were already burning.

Rosa put her hands on her hips and gave me a perplexed look. "I don't know what is going on between you and your husband, but you need to put that aside because we need his help now. Go down to his bar and get Marco or I will."

"I'm telling you we can do this, Rosa. Just bend your knees, get a good grip, and lift on the count of three. Ready? One. Two –"

It was almost ten o'clock when I knocked on the front door of Down the Hatch, Marco's bar, just two buildings down from my shop. The lights were off and there was no sign of activity, but I knew he was in there; we'd driven downtown together. I just didn't know what kind of mood I'd find him in.

"It looks like the Grinch's lair in there," Rosa said, peering into the darkened glass between her gloved hands.

"Tell me about it," I said and knocked again. As I waited for him to open the door, I glanced around. The entire square sparkled with brilliant red, green and gold decorations, shop windows abounded with Christmas candles, awnings were decorated with dangling doves, and red-wrapped wreaths hung from the fronts of doors. Then there was Marco's bar. The black hole of Christmas cheer.

Rosa turned to me and asked the question that I knew had been on everyone's mind. "What happened between you and Marco? You haven't been yourself all morning."

I sighed, feeling the start of tears. "Same thing that happened last year."

"What happened last year?"

"All I can tell you is that for some reason Marco and Christmas don't get along. I made the mistake of asking him why, but he wouldn't answer." I wiped away a stray tear. "I don't know how to reach him."

She pounded on the door, trying to get his attention. "Maybe he will tell me why."

Good luck with that, I thought.

"Morning, ladies," Marco greeted from behind us as if our earlier disagreement had never taken place. He was holding a paper coffee cup, steaming in the cold morning air.

"Marco, you must come help us," Rosa said. "*Vamonos!*"

"What's going on?"

"We have twenty-four iron stands and twenty-four pots of poinsettias to deliver and we are already late," Rosa explained. "We need your help."

He wiggled his key into the front door with his free hand. "No problem," he said casually. "Where exactly are we delivering them?"

"Santa's Village at Churchill's," Rosa answered, and instantly Marco's body tensed.

"We must be quick," Rosa continued. "Bring your coffee and come. We are late already."

"Nope. Sorry." He opened the door and stepped inside, dropping his keys onto the long, polished wood bar that filled the left side of the room. "I'm not going anywhere near that place."

"Why?" Rosa asked as we followed him into the darkened bar.

"Because I can't, that's why."

"That is not a reason," Rosa said.

"Rosa, let's go," I said.

"You want to know my reason?" Marco asked. "The Christmas carols, the shopping, the needy kids, the pushy parents. . ." He stopped and let out a long, frustrated sigh, running his fingers through the sides of his hair. "It's too much for me, that's all."

"But that is *Christmas*," Rosa said with a puzzled frown.

"You can have it," Marco muttered.

"In other words," I said to Rosa, "bah, humbug."

Marco stopped to take a drink of his coffee. "If you want to put it that way," he said, "yes. Bah, humbug."

"Okay, I get that you don't like Christmas," Rosa said, "but think of it this way. All we need is twenty minutes to make a delivery. Maybe thirty, but you do not have to step inside the building."

Marco stood there sipping his coffee, unwavering in his decision, his behavior so unlike my handsome hero that he felt like a stranger to me.

"Forget it, Rosa," I said, giving him a scowl. "We'll manage by ourselves."

"*Santa Madre de Dios,*" Rosa cried, finally losing her patience. "What is wrong with a man who would not want to help his own wife?"

He grabbed his keys from the bar and started toward the door. "Let's get this over with."

CHAPTER TWO

Rosa pulled out of the alley in our bright green *Bloomers Flower Shop* delivery van and drove us toward Churchill's. It was quite a sight to behold, even that early in the morning. Just outside of the department store's main entrance was a scene straight out of a movie. The street was blocked on both sides of the building. Oversized candy canes and ornaments decorated the sidewalks. On the frosted courthouse lawn facing the store was a gigantic Christmas tree that stretched as high as the courthouse clock tower. Next to the tree was Santa's sleigh being led by eight plastic reindeer, and alongside was a pathway marked by golden stanchions strung together with thick red rope, leading straight into the store.

Already, children and parents, bundled in thick winter gear were beginning to form a line that extended out into the street. It had been a long-standing tradition that every Christmas Eve morning at ten on the nose, Santa would exit his indoor workshop, drawing a large crowd to Santa's Village at the back of the store, right next to their two-story Christmas tree. Santa was always played by Mr. Churchill himself, sitting in his big red and gold chair in front of a tiny, brightly painted workshop. He would sit the children on his lap and make a big show of checking his list twice, and then hand out gifts, the most expensive ones first until they were all gone.

I could remember waiting in that line as a child. My parents and I would stand outside in the freezing cold and then slowly wind our way through the warm building, with me shedding layer by layer until my dad was holding all but my snow pants and undershirt. My dad would tease me about being on the naughty list, but I never was. Although the other kids would be cranky and tired, I was always eager and wide awake. I couldn't wait to see Santa.

Churchill's department store had been family-owned for generations, but Levi Churchill took the holiday to a whole new level. After his wife died, he became wrapped up in the role of Santa Claus, even going so far as to grow a full beard and put on a few extra pounds to look the part. He seemed to be comforted by his role and was no longer content being confined inside the department store. He got the whole town involved.

The jubilant tradition that was formed from Churchill's tragedy was the New Chapel square Christmas Eve celebration. Once the sun had set, Santa would come outside to sit in his sleigh while the whole town turned out to count down the annual lighting of the star on top of the Christmas tree. It gave joy to Churchill, brought business back into the town square, and became a treasured memory for me and my family. I was thrilled to be a part of it again.

Rosa turned the van into the alley behind Churchill's where a tall, older woman wearing oval, black-rimmed glasses, a festive red dress, and, what I could only describe as a modern beehive hairdo, stepped out of the delivery door to meet us. She had the van's back doors opened before we could even exit the vehicle and, without any introduction, immediately began reading off a list of instructions.

Rosa passed beside her with a dismissive wave of her hand. "We know what to do, Marcille," she said in a surprisingly rude tone. "Move out of our way and let us work."

"You're just lucky Mr. Churchill is running late," Marcille snipped back, "or you'd be in real trouble." She repositioned her glasses on her face and peered down at her clipboard. "He wants two dozen poinsettias lined up ten feet apart starting at the east door and ending at Santa's Workshop." She looked up from the clipboard to make sure we were listening. "And by the way, the east door is the main entrance."

Rosa halted with her back to Marcille and rolled her shoulders to ease her tension. "I *know* where the main entrance is."

Ignoring Rosa, Marcille said, "Mr. Churchill also specifically requested a poinsettia be placed on the left and right side of Santa's throne."

"His throne?" I had to hide my chuckle.

Marcille's big bug eyes flashed angrily. "Excuse me? What did you just say?"

"His throne," I said. "Like he's a king. It's just a funny way to —"

"What would you call it then, Ms. Knight?"

"I'd call it Santa's chair, and it's Mrs. Salvare, not Ms. Knight."

"Is it now?" Marcille removed her glasses and clapped the clipboard against her side. "When I came to your little shop to place this order, the sign above the door read, *Abby Knight, proprietor,* so I suggest if you don't like being called Ms. Knight, you have the sign changed."

She wasn't wrong – it was something I'd been meaning to change since my wedding several months earlier – but my Irish temper began to manifest itself through a blush on my cheeks, making my freckles stand out all the more. I drew in a deep breath, reminding myself what day it was, and decided my best move was to ignore her.

Marco, Rosa, and I carried the wrought iron stands and flowers through the delivery door and placed them just inside. After inspecting each one, Marcille said, "I'll let Mr. Churchill know you're setting up," and walked off, leaving Rosa muttering a few Spanish obscenities at her retreating back.

"Who is Marcille and what's her problem?" I asked, as I set my jacket on the ground and rolled up my sleeves. The store was just as warm and toasty as I'd remembered.

"Marcille Shelby. She thinks she is God because she is the store manager," Rosa said, wrinkling her nose. "She was my boss when I worked at the perfume counter, and it didn't take long before I came to despise her."

"Okay," Marco said, wiping the dirt from his hands. "My work here is done."

"*Por favor, no!* You cannot go yet," Rosa begged. "You do not know this man like I do. If everything is not perfect, Abby will never get Churchill's business again."

"You promised that I wouldn't have to enter the building."

"Please, Marco?" I asked. "I could really use his business. Just give us fifteen more minutes and we'll take it from there."

Marco breathed in deeply, as he always did when he didn't want to do something. "Fine, fifteen minutes, but that's it."

As Marco went back to the delivery door to pick up some stands, I had a quick chat with Rosa as we followed behind with the flowers. "Tell me," I teased, "what's so bad about Marcille? Other than her personality and manners, she seemed perfectly nice to me."

"You joke about this woman, but I tell you she has the devil in her. She is even more strict with the employees than Levi Churchill. I despise her. When I worked for her she would make me go home and change clothing. She was always jealous of me."

As Rosa leaned down to place a poinsettia, I studied her outfit. Even her thick winter jacket somehow managed to expose her curves. After months of pondering Rosa's clothing choices, I couldn't help but understand Marcille's concerns.

We continued to work quickly, Marco arranging the stands and Rosa and I filling them with poinsettias, doing our best to ignore the long line of impatient children and grumbling parents who were waiting for Santa's arrival. In no time at all, the three of us had created a beautiful path to Santa's Village, and there was still no sign of Levi Churchill.

"Let's go," said Marco. "We're done here."

"We'll meet you at the van. Rosa and I still need to decorate around Santa's chair."

As Marco headed for the delivery door, I looked in awe at the surroundings. We were directly in the middle of the store, with shops all around us. Somewhat smaller than I remembered, yet still cute, Santa's Village was situated near the rear of the main floor. There were child-sized gingerbread men and giant nutcrackers standing alongside Santa's red and gold chair. Leading up to the chair was a red carpet sprinkled generously with fake snow.

Directly behind Santa's big chair was his bright green workshop, where elves would soon come out to distribute peppermint candy canes. The back entrance to the workshop was just steps away from the elevator so that Levi Churchill could come down and secretly enter the tiny shack, change into his suit, and emerge as Santa Claus from a red door in front. To the right of the workshop was a two-story Christmas tree decorated with tinsel, glass ornaments, and candy canes. The tree extended up into the second floor, where shoppers and children could admire the full scene from the circular balcony.

Visiting Santa's Village had always been a magical time for me as a child, waiting in that long line, anticipating what toy the jovial Santa would pull from his giant red bag while Christmas carols played in the background. A chill of excitement ran up my spine.

"Excuse me, Miss," came an impatient male voice from the crowd. "Do you know what's taking Santa so long?"

A young-looking mother standing several families behind him, rocking a large sleeping child in her arms, added, "We've been waiting over an hour already."

"I'm sorry. I don't work here." I turned to whisper to Rosa, "Where are the elves? Shouldn't they be handing out candy canes to pacify the children?"

"I don't know," she whispered back, "but it's not our problem. Let's just finish and get out of here."

Dodging the annoying looks and increasingly rude remarks of the waiting families, we placed the last two perfect poinsettias beside Santa's chair and stepped back to regard our work. Next to the chair sat a giant red bag filled to the brim with perfectly-wrapped presents. Everything was set up and ready to go, but still there was no sign of Santa. I checked the time. It was now thirty minutes past ten.

A well-dressed woman standing first in line was holding the hand of a boy I guessed to be about five years old who waited patiently at her side. "Do you have any idea what time it is?" she asked us rhetorically.

"I don't work here," I told her. "I'm just the florist."

She huffed impatiently as the boy gazed at me with big, sweet, blue eyes. The woman huffed again to regain my attention. "Santa was supposed to be here promptly at ten and my son is becoming very impatient."

"I'm sorry. I wish I could help."

"You *can* help. Check the workshop. Do *something!*"

I looked around at all of the various departments where employees were helping the customers not standing in line. I glanced up to the second floor, the balcony level, its brass railing strung with braids of red tinsel. That level, filled with shops for men, was also bustling with activity. The store seemed to be humming along beautifully, but why hadn't Santa or his elves shown up?

My inner radar began beeping. "Something doesn't feel right, Rosa. I'm going to have a look around."

"Let's just get out of here," Rosa said glancing around nervously. "I'm sure Marco has the van ready to go."

"I don't think so." I pointed across the room to the toy department where, to my utter surprise, Marco was standing near a display of toy footballs. Perhaps he'd been drawn in by the music and had finally let in some of the Christmas spirit. Or, more likely, he'd simply grown tired of waiting and had come inside to shag us out. I was betting on the latter.

Before we were married, Marco had confessed his dislike of Christmas to me, just in case it was a deal-breaker. It hadn't been, but I'd had no idea how deep that dislike went. He still celebrated with our families, but in a quiet, almost withdrawn way, yet he was never around when I put up the tree, couldn't stand to hear my old holiday records, and wouldn't explain why. That's what really bothered me. Marco and I told each other everything, so why not that?

Our most recent argument on that subject had begun on our drive to work that morning when I'd casually mentioned that he should join me at the Bloomers booth for the Christmas Eve celebration. His curt reply left me hurt and stunned. I couldn't fathom why anyone could be so anti-Christmas, so I had to keep telling myself to be patient and let Marco open up to me when the time was right. Unfortunately for me, patience was not a virtue.

And neither was it for the woman standing first in line. "Hello? Ms. Florist? You said you were going to help."

"That's it," I said to Rosa. "I'm going in."

"No, Abby," Rosa held my arm. "Do not get involved. Something is very wrong. We will find Marcille."

"I'll just knock and see what happens. Maybe it's nothing at all." But my gut was telling me a different story.

"Then I am coming with you."

I walked across the pad of fake snow that had been laid out all around Santa's Village and knocked on the red door.

Looking back, I could see all the way down the line to the front entrance where children peered around their siblings and parents craned their necks, impatiently waiting to find out what was happening.

There was no answer so I knocked again, then tried the door handle and found it unlocked. I pulled the wooden door open and a young girl's pale arm flopped out onto the fake snow in front of me.

"Call 911," I told Rosa. "Tell them we need an ambulance, fast."

CHAPTER THREE

I squeezed through the door of the little wooden shack and knelt by the young girl's side, putting my fingers to her throat to feel for a pulse. She seemed no older than sixteen and was dressed in a bright red and green elf costume. I took off my coat and covered her, then pulled the hat from her head, causing her eyelids to flutter briefly. At least she was alive, her pulse strong. "Rosa," I called. "Get Marco and then keep a watch out for the paramedics. Oh, and tell them to use the back door."

"*Sí*, I will go get your husband right now."

Marco opened the back door almost immediately. As soon as he saw me kneeling beside the young girl he asked, "What happened?"

"I don't know yet. Help me get her inside. She's hurt."

He stopped suddenly and stepped over a small puddle of semi-dried blood, brushing his head against the lone light bulb dangling from the ceiling, casting odd shadows around the terrifying scene.

The room was tall but not wide, just big enough for two folding chairs and a small wooden end table. It wouldn't have been a comfortable changing room, but I noticed some clothes hanging in the corner. There were no decorations, just two-by-fours with nails sticking out acting as hooks. Candy canes littered the floor around us and one of the chairs had been upturned. Marco knelt next to me and we helped the stunned girl sit upright. She held the back of her head and mumbled a few words before she finally snapped to.

"What happened?" the girl asked groggily, rubbing the back of her skull.

"We don't know yet," I said, kneeling beside her. "Can you tell me your name?"

"Hailey," she said, struggling to sit upright.

"Just lie still, Hailey. You've suffered a blow to your head and we're getting you some help."

"Abby." Marco pointed to a big dent in the doorframe which led me to believe that she had hit her head pretty hard before falling against the door.

"Hailey," I asked, "can you turn your head for me?"

Still groggy, she eased it to one side, where I saw a small trickle of blood coming from the back of her scalp. From the location of the wound, it looked as if she'd either tripped and fallen backward or been pushed against the door.

I could hear Rosa outside telling people to move out of the way, and a moment later she poked her head in through the front door. "The ambulance is on its way. Is the girl all right?"

"She's doing okay," I said.

At that, Hailey turned her head, her gaze unfocused. "Where's my dad?" She looked around the tiny room and saw the blood on the floor. She began to panic. That's when I noticed an envelope under a pile of broken candy canes by the baseboard. Before I could pick it up, the girl frantically asked again, "Where is my dad?"

Marco and I lifted Hailey to her feet, helped her out of the back door, carefully avoiding the pool of blood, and sat her on a soft pad of fake snow. Rosa met us behind the house and her eyes grew large. She grabbed my arm to pull me away, whispering in my ear, "That is Levi Churchill's daughter."

From the other side of Santa's workshop, we could hear people crying, "Where is Santa. We want Santa!"

"Have you seen him?" Hailey asked, her voice rising in panic. "He was here when I left to get the candy canes." She looked at her hand, covered in fresh blood from her head wound, and cried, "What happened?"

"We don't know yet," I replied. "Rosa, will you see what you can do about quieting the crowd? Or find Marcille and have her do it."

"Tell us what you remember, Hailey," Marco said as he crouched beside the frightened teenager.

She gazed at him warily. "Who are you?"

"My name is Marco Salvare. I'm a private detective and this is my wife, Abby. Can you tell me what you remember about this morning?"

She sniffled back tears, her lower lip trembling. "Dad was getting ready to change into his Santa suit so I went upstairs to get the candy canes from his office. When I came back down, he was gone. That's all I remember." She wiped her eyes with her sleeve.

"Did anything seem out of the ordinary?" Marco asked. "Was your dad acting differently?"

"No, he was excited," she began to sniffle again, "and I was so mean." At that, she wept openly. "I'm so sorry for everything I said to him."

I held her close, rocking her back and forth to comfort her. Although I didn't have any children, my motherly instincts were strong – but my detective instincts were even stronger – probably because I didn't have any children. I needed to get back into that room and find out what was in the envelope before the police showed up. I ran my hand down the back of her head, avoiding the wound, and smoothed out her hair. "Do you remember how you hit your head?" I asked.

She sniffled again and said no.

"Did anyone else come into the workshop while you were there?"

"I don't think so."

"Where are the other elves?" I asked, thinking one of them might have noticed something strange going on.

"I'm the only one this year. Dad had to cut back on his employees." She licked her lips. "Can you get me some water, please?"

There were a few bottles of water scattered on the table inside Santa's workshop. I entered and immediately went for the envelope on the floor. It was an opened legal envelope with the title *CHURCHILL'S LAST CHRISTMAS* typed across the center. There was no stamp, no return address, and no name on it. There was, however, half of a bloody fingerprint on the backside of the envelope. I squeezed it open but the letter had been removed.

I snapped a few photos with my phone, placed the envelope back on the floor, and quickly searched the pants hanging from one of the nails. Inside the back pocket was Churchill's thick leather wallet with his cash, driver's license, and credit cards still folded and secured neatly inside. That wasn't a good sign.

I was careful to avoid the small puddle of blood but noticed a footprint smearing the blood across the floor in one smooth streak. There were several drops also leading out the back entrance and onto the pad of snow before trailing off toward the elevator. I made a mental note to check that out.

"The paramedics and the police are here, Abby," Marco called. "We need to clear out of their way."

I grabbed the water from the table, opened the cap, and returned to Hailey. "Is there anything else you remember before the accident?" I asked. "Anything at all?"

She shook her head and then winced in pain before sipping from the water bottle.

"If you think of anything else," I told her, "make sure you let the police know."

Marco joined me as we watched the paramedics place a thick brace around Hailey's neck and lift her onto the gurney. He kneeled next to us and put his arm around me as I put my hand onto hers.

"Promise me you'll find my dad," she said, then squeezed my hand as if she didn't want to leave.

"We'll find your dad," I said. "I promise."

Before they could roll her away she raised herself on her elbows and called, "Wait, I *did* see something strange, a woman standing by the back door just after I left to get the candy. I didn't get a good look at her, but she was holding something in her hands. It was definitely strange."

"What did she look like?" I asked.

"Sir, Ma'am, you'll have to step back and let us do our job," one of the paramedics said, and then gently positioned her back onto the gurney.

Marco let go of my hand and pointed at the gurney. "Look at her foot."

On the bottom of her green elfin shoe cover was a dark stain. "Is that blood?"

He nodded. "Looks like it."

Before I could tell Marco what I had found inside the house, Sergeant Reilly began calling out instructions for his officers to cordon off the entire Santa's Village to keep the customers away. He walked up to us, his arms folded across his chest, shaking his head at me. "I don't know why I'm surprised to see you here, Abby."

"Good to see you, too, Sarge."

A tall, pleasant looking, brown-haired man, Sean Reilly had helped us out on many of our cases, usually with great reluctance. "Marco," Reilly said as the two men shook hands.

Sergeant Sean Reilly and my husband had been buddies since Marco's brief stint on the New Chapel police force, a career he'd learned was not for him. My husband was a man who played by his own rules, which hadn't made him a good fit as a cop but made him a perfect fit for this feisty, red-headed florist.

"Who found the girl?" Reilly asked.

"I did," I said.

"Of course you did." Reilly flipped open a notepad and retrieved a small pen from his shirt pocket. "Tell me what happened."

As I began to list off the events, I noticed Reilly's men start to tape off Santa's chair, quickly closing in on the workshop. A few more minutes and my investigation would be squelched. I needed to get back there and follow that trail. "And that's about it. I'm sure I'll remember more, but for now, that should be good."

"Are you sure?" Sgt. Reilly asked. "That's it?"

"For now that's it," I answered.

Reilly gave me a suspicious glance. "If you say so."

I gave Marco's hand a quick tug as he began his statement. "I'll be right back," I whispered.

Before I could take two steps, Reilly said, "Hold on a minute. Where are you going?"

I swung around, pasting an innocent look on my face. "To the ladies' room."

"The ladies' room is that way," Reilly informed me, pointing his pen in the opposite direction.

Oops.

"I know you, Abby Salvare," he continued. "What aren't you telling me?"

Okay, so I didn't have a very good poker face, but I did have a very good bluff. "Fine. There's an envelope inside Santa's workshop that looks suspicious. Also, some clothes are hanging inside that might belong to Churchill. I'd like to go back in and check it out."

That was not my actual plan, but Reilly didn't need to know.

"No deal," Reilly said. "The detectives will take care of that when they get here. That's what detectives are hired to do, remember?"

"I get it, Reilly, but by the time your detectives get here, Churchill could be in serious trouble, or worse, dead."

"Why do you assume he's in trouble?" Reilly asked. "Maybe he just got sick and went home. My focus right now is finding out what happened to Hailey Churchill."

I scowled at him for refusing to take me seriously. "Hailey Churchill slipped on a puddle of blood and hit her head on the doorframe. Case closed. Now we have to find out where that puddle of blood came from."

Marco took my hand between his. "Sunshine, calm down. Reilly and his men are on the case." He gave my hand a quick squeeze which meant one thing: Team Salvare was also on the case!

The officers had just finished taping off Santa's chair and were proceeding to the workshop. I had to move quickly. "Go ahead and give him your statement, Marco. I'm going to the ladies' room – and this time don't you dare try to stop me, Reilly."

"Then don't you dare go snooping around, Salvare."

"You know me, Sarge." Ignoring his glare, I gave him a shrug and walked away, in the right direction this time.

There was still a crowd of people standing just outside of the Santa's Village area, some being questioned by police officers, others craning their necks to see what was going on inside. The store employees were standing in front of their departments talking in huddles, not having much to do now that most of the customers had left, and still the Christmas carols played on. Oddly, I had yet to see any sign of Marcille. Why wasn't the store manager around to oversee the situation?

I carefully avoided Reilly's line of sight as I ducked back behind Santa's workshop. The blood drops trailed out from the back door and stopped at the elevator. From there he could only have gone up to the third floor since the second floor was full of customers and the store had no basement. The only problem with that theory was the sign on the elevator door that read, *Out of Order*.

There was only one other quick way to get out. To my left was a short hallway that led to the back stairwell, and under the glare of the overhead fluorescent lights, I could see a faint trail of blood. I followed the trail down to the end of the hallway. Adjacent to the stairwell was an emergency exit where Churchill could have been evacuated. There was a sign on the door that read, *Caution – Alarm Will Sound*, so I avoided pushing my luck. The last thing I needed was to sound an alarm and alert the entire department store to my location.

I headed back toward the elevator, thinking over what I'd seen. There was one blood trail that led to a broken elevator and one that led to an emergency exit. I was stumped. Where could Santa be other than somewhere in the store? Either that or he had risen straight up through the chimney, just like in the poem, except that there was no chimney at Churchill's.

I was about to return to Marco's side when I heard a loud ding and watched as the elevator doors opened in front of me. To my surprise, Marcille walked out, giving me a seething glare from above the rim of her glasses. "You make a better door than a florist," she snapped, sidestepping me.

She moved past me and made her way toward the police, her high heels clicking on the floor before she stopped in front of an officer and demanded to know what was happening. I glanced back as the elevator doors slid closed. Out of order? Not hardly.

CHAPTER FOUR

"There you are," Rosa exclaimed. "Your husband said you were in the bathroom, but I checked and you were not there. Come, I have someone you should talk to."

By that time the whole Santa's Village area had been taped off, with several policemen standing guard. Only a few customers remained, including the woman and the little boy who'd been first in line to see Santa. The woman was standing in front of the toy department where her son was gazing wistfully at a toy football on a display stand, just as Marco had done earlier.

"Abby Salvare, this is Rhonda the Saddler," Rosa said. "Rhonda has some information you need to hear."

"It's Rhondella Saddler," the woman corrected, "and as I said, I saw an old woman at the back door of Santa's Workshop who definitely didn't belong there."

"Why do you say she didn't belong there?" I asked.

"Mommy," her son said, pointing at the football.

"Hush, Thomas. Not now." Turning back to me, Rhondella said, "For one thing, she didn't have any children with her. For another, she was wearing Jimmy Choo high heels and wore at least a grand in diamonds on each ear lobe. Any woman wearing that kind of bling at a children's Christmas celebration is definitely up to no good."

"Mommy?"

She gave his arm a sharp tug. "I said not *now*, Thomas! Ladies, you'll have to excuse us. This has been a sorely disappointing day, and my child is extremely restless."

She was the one who looked restless to me. And the poor boy looked ready to cry.

"Would you at least tell me approximately how old the woman was?" I asked as Rosa bent down to calm the child.

"You know what I mean, *old*," Rhondella replied, wrinkling her nose in distaste. "Not hunched back, using-a-walker old, but white-haired, wrinkly-skinned old."

Rosa glanced up in disgust at her insensitive remarks and muttered something in Spanish.

"What did you say to me?" Rhondella challenged.

"She was asking what time you saw the woman," I said quickly.

"It was early. Not as early as us, but definitely before ten. In fact, we skipped breakfast this morning so we would have first dibs on the extra special gifts. Santa always puts the best gifts on top of his sack. And even though he never showed up" -she pulled a wrapped present from her oversized purse- "I grabbed one anyway."

"You didn't give your son breakfast?" Rosa turned back to the child and took one of his hands in hers. "Poor little niño, you must be starving. You know what? I have a snack bar in my purse you can have."

"Oh, no. He's fine." Rhondella pulled her son's hand from Rosa's, keeping him firmly by her side. "He had a few candy canes that were in a bowl by the front door. Come, Thomas, we must be going."

And with that, she led her son down the hallway and turned the corner.

"Do you believe that *bruja*?" Rosa asked. "What a terrible way to treat her little boy."

"I'm with you. She was so rude, I had a hard time concentrating on what she was saying."

"Do not worry. I have it all right here," Rosa tapped her forehead. "I never forget anything."

Marco came striding up to meet us, a look of weary relief in his eyes. "It's been much longer than thirty minutes. I think we should be going now."

Back at Bloomers, the morning rush had diminished to just a few customers chatting over tea and scones in the attached coffee and tea parlor. I could smell the aroma of baked goods wafting in from the parlor and my stomach, which had been on hold all morning, immediately started growling. Rosa must have heard it because she gave me a wink and was off to the kitchen to whip up a quick batch of her *huevos*.

I glanced around my little shop with pride. Having flunked out of law school my first year, with no prospects in sight, I'd been given a new lease on life when Lottie decided to sell Bloomers to me. Using the last bit of money my grandfather had left me, I'd taken out a mortgage and hired Lottie back as my assistant. I could hear her now humming in the workroom, doing what she loved best, creating arrangements with no worries about finances.

And then there was Grace Bingham, a native Brit in her mid-sixties with a knack for efficiently running my coffee-and-tea parlor. She made the best scones in town, and always had a quote at the ready for every situation. Finding her had been a stroke of pure luck. Grace stepped nimbly from the parlor, dressed as usual in a black skirt with a matching sweater set, this one in red for the season.

Before I could even say hello, Jillian began explaining how she had single-handedly saved Bloomers from the morning rush disaster. It wasn't until she'd finished that she asked me to describe what had happened at Churchill's.

"Yes, love," Grace seconded. "Please regale us. We heard there was quite an uproar."

Lottie swiped open the curtain, still in her yellow apron, and joined us by the register.

I took my coat off and hung it behind the counter. "Santa Claus is missing and his daughter was knocked unconscious as a result. That's all we know for sure."

"Santa Claus has a daughter?" Jillian asked.

Sometimes it was hard to believe Jillian had graduated from Harvard. "Not Santa," I explained, "Levi Churchill. You know, the man who dresses up to play Santa every year? His daughter, Hailey, was dressed up as an elf. We think she slipped on a puddle of blood and hit her head."

"Good heavens," Grace said.

I took a seat on the tall stool behind the register and Marco gave me a tap of his watch. His bar opened in fifteen minutes for the lunch crowd and we had information to swap. Team Salvare was still firing on all cylinders, without even a word spoken, and in the middle of an unsettled Christmas Eve argument, no less.

"First," I said. "I want to hear what Marco learned from Sergeant Reilly."

"He wouldn't tell me much," Marco stated, "other than that he's not concerned about Churchill at this point. He's convinced the blood on the floor is from Hailey's head wound, so that's the focus of their investigation right now."

"Surely Sergeant Reilly can see the sense of considering Levi Churchill to be a missing person," Grace said. "He wouldn't have just left without telling anyone."

"Not in a Santa suit," Lottie said. "Someone would've seen him." She grabbed a white vase from the wall near us and made her way back to the workroom.

"Unfortunately," Marco continued, "it takes forty-eight hours before the police consider this to be a missing persons case, and from what Reilly indicated, there's no proof that any harm has come to him. So unless they find proof, they intend to wait the full forty-eight hours, and that's *only* if a family member comes forward to file a report."

"That's why Marco and I are going to look for him," I said. "I gave my word to Hailey that I'd find her dad and I intend to keep that promise."

"What about tonight?" Jillian asked. "The Christmas Eve celebration starts in…" She checked her white and silver watch, then shook her arm and listened for a tick.

"Just over six hours," I finished. "The celebration starts at six o'clock. Workers are still out there setting up so it looks like everything will continue as planned."

"It won't be Christmas Eve without Churchill," Grace said. "How could they possibly proceed without him?"

"If I know Churchill," Rosa stated as she set a big plate of eggs and several forks on the counter, "and believe me, I do, the celebration will proceed with or without him as long as the store is open and making money." She spiked her fork into the eggs and took a mouthful. "Marcille will make sure of that."

Marco looked at me and continued, "I don't know if you managed to sneak your way into the workshop, but that envelope you mentioned could be a very important clue."

"I did, actually. Before Reilly told me not to, I went in and snapped a few photos." I pulled out my phone and let him swipe through the pictures. "But that's not all. I also searched through the pants hanging on the hook and found Churchill's wallet. The money and credit cards were still there, so he wasn't robbed."

"And he wouldn't leave the area without his wallet," Marco added, handing me back my phone. "What do you think *Churchill's Last Christmas* means?"

"Churchill's last what?" Lottie called from the workroom.

"Last Christmas," I repeated. "It sounds like a threat to me. It was typed out on a legal envelope, but the letter inside was missing. And there was half of a bloody fingerprint on the envelope, which could mean the other half is on the letter itself. We need to find it."

"The fingerprint could be tested for DNA," Jillian said. "I've seen that on TV. That's how all these cases are solved nowadays, with high-technicians."

"Hi-tech," I said. My cousin drove me crazy with her misuse of words.

Marco shot her idea down. "It takes weeks to have DNA tested."

"That's why I'm saying we need to investigate now, Marco. Churchill could be dead by then." Seeing the defeated look on Jillian's face, I added, "But that was a good thought, Jill."

"What about the woman wearing the expensive jewelry?" Rosa asked.

I stopped to swallow a bite of egg. "First, I should mention that Hailey told me she saw a woman standing by the back door of Santa's Workshop just before Churchill went missing. Then Rosa and I spoke to someone who also saw a woman near the back door wearing expensive heels and jewelry. If this is the same woman, she could either be a potential witness, or better yet, a suspect in Churchill's disappearance." I caught my husband's frown and asked, "Don't you agree?"

"Assuming this woman, wearing heels and expensive jewelry, had the strength to attack and carry out a large man in a Santa suit with no one noticing," Marco said dryly, "it's a good theory."

"Hailey said she was holding something," I countered. "Maybe it was a gun."

"Maybe," Marco said. "But Hailey would've recognized a gun."

"Fine," I said, "we'll cross her off as a suspect for now. Rosa, since you worked there, you know the Churchill family better than we do. Can you think of anyone who'd want to hurt Levi Churchill?"

"*Si,*" she said. "The employees were always complaining. He was never afraid to fire someone on the spot. And he was very stingy with his raises."

"That narrows it down," Marco said, crossing his arms.

"It's hard to believe Churchill would be that kind of a boss. I remember him being so jolly and kind," I said as I cleaned up my plate full of eggs.

"After his wife died he threw all of his energy into the business," Rosa said. "He believes this town would suffer without him. The power has gone straight to his head."

Grace went into her lecture pose, shoulders straight, fingers laced in front of her. "As Abraham Lincoln once said, 'Nearly all men can stand adversity, but if you want to test a man's character, give him power.'"

"Good quote, Gracie," Lottie said, coming out of the workroom with a bouquet overflowing with holly and mistletoe. "And I agree with you, Abby. It's hard to believe Churchill has turned into that kind of man. I remember taking my boys to see Santa every year. But that was fifteen years ago. A lot can happen in fifteen years."

"What a beautiful arrangement," Jillian said, sniffing the holly. "Who's it for?"

"This," Lottie answered, turning the bouquet so we could see, "is for Hailey. I had a feeling Abby might be going to the hospital to visit her. We ordered a bunch of these flowers for our Christmas booth tonight," Lottie reminded me. "With Churchill missing and things in chaos, I sure hope we'll be able to sell them."

I'd become so wrapped up in what had happened at Churchill's that I'd totally forgotten about our booth on the town square. "I'm sure people will still turn out this evening. The celebration is a long-standing tradition."

Marco slipped on his jacket. "How about after the lunch rush at the bar, Abby, you and I visit Hailey and see if she's able to give us more information? So far all we have is a missing letter and a mystery woman, and that's not very promising. We need a solid lead."

"Oh, wait! I may have one," I said. "While you were talking to Reilly I followed a trail of blood drops leading straight toward the elevator. There was a sign attached to it that said *Out of Order*. And then who should walk out of that very elevator? Marcille, the snooty store manager."

"So she knew the elevator was working," Marco said.

"Maybe she had one of the employees force Santa into the elevator," Rosa proposed. "I tell you, there are many people at that store who have grudges against him."

"Then before our hospital visit," I said to Marco, "I'm going back to the department store to ask Marcille a few questions."

"Not alone," Marco said. "We don't know who we're dealing with."

"I will go with her," Rosa offered. "Remember, I saved her life when she was stuck in that maze of yews. Jillian can stay here and help Lottie, can't you, Jillian?"

"I'd be happy to."

Just then the bells jingled above Bloomers' front door and in walked my parents, Maureen "Mad Mo" Knight and my dad, Jeffery Knight. My dad, a retired sergeant of the New Chapel police department, was in a wheelchair after having sustained a debilitating injury on the job, causing him to live out the rest of his life as a paraplegic. His spirits had never suffered, though. He was a great man and I adored him.

My mother was pretty amazing herself, with seemingly endless energy and a creative drive that never ceased to impress me. The art projects she'd created, on the other hand, were something else entirely. The word *nightmare* sprang to mind.

I sighed as my mom held up a large garment bag. *What nightmare had she made now?*

CHAPTER FIVE

"How's my Abracadabra?" my dad asked, using my childhood nickname.

I gave him and Mom a hug. "I'm fine. What are you two up to?"

"Your mother couldn't wait to show you what she made for tonight," Dad said.

"Abigail," Mom chimed, "you're going to love this."

I forced myself to smile. "I can't wait."

As Mom began to unload her bag, I noticed Grace had nimbly backed into the tea parlor, and the purple curtain separating the workroom was now closed, with Rosa, Lottie, and our breakfast dishes suspiciously missing. It was just Jillian, Marco, and me.

"Marco, my boy," Dad said, "how about you and I go grab some beers at Down The Hatch and watch the holiday bowl game?"

"Sorry," Marco said, "no football at my bar today. You'll have to excuse me," he said to both of my parents. "I've got to open for lunch."

"Hold up a minute," Dad said. "No football on Christmas Eve, again? How can you hope to attract customers without having the game on?"

"Believe it or not," Marco said stiffly, "not everyone likes football." He zipped up his jacket. "It was good to see you both. Abby, I'll be here at one-thirty and we can head over to the hospital." And then he stalked out.

My dad shook his head, clearly as perplexed by Marco's attitude as I was. "What kind of man doesn't celebrate Christmas *and* hates football? What happens when you have children? Are you just going to skip Christmas?"

"Dad, leave Marco to me. He'll come around."

"In the meantime," he said, "here I am the day before Christmas with no game to watch."

"You won't have time for football anyway," Mom said as she pulled the first garment out of her bag. "We need to go set up our booth for tonight." She held the outfit up to her chin, an oversized red and white Mrs. Claus costume, complete with a dainty ruffled collar and cuffs and a stuffed muffin-top bonnet. "What do you think?"

Jillian clapped her hands together in delight. "I love it! You'll have to make me one, Aunt Mo."

"I can do that. I made Abby's father a costume, too."

"Don't tell me," I said. "A Santa Claus suit."

"You didn't tell me your parents had a booth tonight," Jillian said to me. "What are you selling, Aunt Maureen?"

"My latest children's mystery book, Christmas-themed, of course. You'll love it, Jillian, and you can read it to your little Harper, too. Are you girls ready for the title?"

As ready as I'd ever be.

"It's A Wonderful *Leaf*," Mom said with a keen smile.

My mouth fell open. It was actually good. "That's really clever, Mom. Isn't it, Jill?" I nudged my cousin who was still trying to figure out the pun.

"Thank you, Abigail," Mom said. "It's not easy coming up with all these flower pun titles." She pulled out my dad's Santa costume to show us. "What do you think of this?"

"Both outfits look fantastic, Mom."

"I'm glad you think so, because I made something for you, too."

Dear God. I reached for something to lean on as Mom pulled out her final costume. It was a short, one-piece, green elf suit, not unlike the costume Hailey Churchill had been wearing, except this one had a very short skirt and bright green and black tights.

Great. I was going to be a twenty-seven-year-old elf in a sixteen-year-old's costume. Just what a five-foot-two, busty redhead needed to make her day complete.

"And just wait until you see the shoes I made for you."

I'd seen enough. "Mom, it all looks incredible and I'm so proud of you, but I think there's something you should know."

I explained what had happened to Churchill and his daughter, filling them in on just enough detail to get me out of elf duty for the evening. "I'm sorry. I really wish I could be there to help, but—"

"I'll wear the elf costume, Aunt Mo," Jillian exclaimed, snatching up the outfit. "I'd love to help, and I can rock this little skirt. What do you think?"

"That's a great idea, Jill," I said.

"No, I meant about the skirt. What do you think?"

"I'd be happy to have you fill in," Mom said, "but don't the Osbornes have their annual Christmas Eve luncheon right about now?"

"Ugh, *Christmas with the Osbornes*. Don't get me started."

"We won't," I said as several customers entered the store accompanied by the festive jingle above their heads.

"Too late," Jillian continued. "I'm already started. I am not spending another Christmas Eve with my in-laws and their stuck-up relations in a drafty old mansion with a real tree that stinks the whole place up like the outdoors. And all they serve is warm wine. Can you even imagine? Harper is with her father right now getting ready, but honestly, I'd rather sit out in the cold wearing an elf costume than stand around making small talk with wealthy artistic rats."

"Aristocrats, Jill."

"We have all day tomorrow to celebrate Christmas with *my* family, a *real* Christmas, with a fake tree and stockings filled with presents just like it should be. I'll miss the yearly Christmas photo, which is a bummer because I look amazing, but I can ask the photographers to Photoshop me in later. Now, when should I change into my costume?"

"Let's go set up the booth first," Mom said. "I have a box of books in the trunk and some cold wine in the back seat." She winked at Jillian and they giggled.

"I guess I'll just be the third wheel, so to speak," Dad pouted.

We heard Grace singing from the tea parlor, "Oh, Jeffery."

My mom, Jillian, and I followed my dad into the parlor where Grace had set up a small portable television in the back near the coffee bar. I could smell the fresh coffee beans brewing as Grace tuned the TV to the football game.

"Now, you relax," Grace said, "while Lottie and I tend to the shop and your wife and niece set up the booth." She took a steaming cup of coffee from the counter and handed it to my dad, who still seemed locked into his bad mood. "Don't drink it too fast. It's quite hot." She leaned down to whisper, "And there's a little extra Irish cheer in it that'll fix you right up."

Finally, my dad cracked a smile.

Noon, Christmas Eve

As Rosa and I headed back to Churchill's, the town square was truly starting to come alive. The streets were still full of shoppers and some of the shop owners were already decorating their booths. We walked past a group of men on the courthouse lawn constructing the portable riser stage for the choir performing that evening. Everything was coming together.

The downtown Christmas Eve celebration had not only been a tradition for the town, but for my family as well. I couldn't imagine Christmas without it. I kept hoping Marco would see the magic in it, too. Unfortunately, I feared that this year, our first Christmas as husband and wife, would be just like the last and he'd spend the evening alone rather than with me.

The long line of people waiting outside of Churchill's had vanished, so we entered through the front doors. "We'll just go in, find Marcille, and get some answers," I said. "We have less than six hours until the celebration, and I want Santa in his sleigh by the time they light that star."

"You leave Marcille to me," Rosa said. "I will find out what she knows."

I wasn't expecting much activity inside, but to my surprise, the department store was busy. We walked down the hall, passing our evenly spaced poinsettias, toward Santa's Village. As we came closer, we noticed the yellow tape had been taken down around the village – the surrounding area now lively and festive, the Christmas music loud and cheerful, and the departments full of shoppers – as though nothing had happened just one hour earlier. Not even a single police officer could be seen.

Even more shocking, a small line of people had begun to form in front of Santa's chair. And then, as if the situation couldn't have gotten any more bewildering, Santa Claus himself stepped out of his workshop and gave a grand, sweeping wave to the growing crowd, causing the kids to cheer with excitement.

I knew at once it wasn't Churchill. On this man, the Santa suit hung loosely from his thin frame and despite the white mustache and beard, I could see a smooth face and youthful eyes. Still, no one seemed to mind.

"What's going on here?" I asked Rosa.

"Something strange," she answered, "because that man is not Levi Churchill."

Then a frightening thought occurred to me and I dashed for the elevator to see if I was right. Rosa caught up to me as I bent down to check for the drops of blood, but they were gone, the floors wiped clean. Someone had completely removed all traces of evidence.

"Rosa, cover for me. I'm going inside the workshop." I crept over the pad of fake snow and eased the back door open. The puddle of blood was gone, the floor was clean, the chairs had been removed, and no clothes were hanging from the hooks. I slipped back outside beside Rosa. "The workshop has been completely cleaned out as if nothing ever happened. Have you seen any sign of Marcille yet?"

"No, but she is around somewhere. I can smell her *apestoso* perfume."

We worked our way around the increasingly crowded store until we ended up back by the elevator. "I'm going to check the second floor," I told her. "You keep looking for Marcille down here." I started for the elevator only to have Rosa grab my arm. "What are you doing? What if it really is out of order?"

"I don't think it is." I pressed the button and the gears of the ancient contraption sprang to life, causing the gold-toned doors to glide open. "I saw Marcille use it earlier – with the sign on it. She didn't seem concerned at all."

Rosa's lips pressed together in anger. "When you find her, bring her to me."

"Okay, it's time to tell me what she did to make you dislike her so much."

"She stole the store manager job from me, that's what she did. She was not happy when I applied for the position because it was obvious that I was better qualified, so she made sure I did not get it."

"How?"

"She made up lies about me."

"What lies?"

"She said horrible things about the way I dress and act. But even worse than that, she said I was not in this country legally even though I had proof. After that, everyone looked at me differently, especially Churchill, and I did not get the job."

With that, she spun around and began the search for Marcille.

Before taking the elevator to the second floor, I decided to retrace my steps to the emergency exit to see if the drops of blood had been wiped clean. Sure enough, they had. In fact, it looked as though the entire area had been mopped, leaving me to wonder who had cleaned it and why. I studied the emergency exit. If only I had the nerve to push open the door and see if the alarm would sound, I could be sure that Churchill was still somewhere in the building.

I hurried back to the elevator and entered, praying that the *Out of Order* sign was false. There was a faint musty smell inside that made me hold my nose. I pressed the button for the second floor and the elevator doors closed. As I began my slow ascent, I tried to imagine what had happened in the workshop that morning.

Santa would have already been dressed in his red suit when someone entered the back way. There wasn't much space inside so there couldn't have been more than one attacker. Had Santa cried out in alarm, and if so, would anyone in that noisy crowd have heard him? The signs pointed to some kind of a struggle, with one chair upturned and a puddle of blood on the floor, but had it been a friendly face that had greeted him at the door or someone with a deep grudge?

I checked the elevator floor for blood stains but there were none. I examined the panel buttons for bloody prints. Still nothing. I bent down and looked under the railing and there it was, the clue I needed – a small swipe of dried blood. As the elevator sounded and the doors slid open, I pulled out my phone and snapped a photo of the blood.

Stepping out, I walked over to the railing encircling the second-floor balcony and placed my hands on the red tinsel braid, gazing down on the main floor. Christmas music echoed throughout the store as laughter and chatter from shoppers below floated upward. Behind me, the men's clothing and shoe departments were crowded with shoppers being helped by busy employees. I was still struck by the fact that everything was proceeding as though nothing unusual had happened. Everyone seemed to be in good spirits. Yet, there was one person who wasn't – Hailey – and that's what mattered to me.

I circulated among the throng until I came to the main stairway opposite the elevator. Several people were walking up and down the stairs with shopping bags, and kids were trying to reach for the large ornaments dangling above their heads, but there was no sign of Marcille. I'd come back to my starting point and looked over the railing when I caught sight of an arm waving at me from below. Rosa was trying to catch my attention. Cupping her hands around her mouth, she called, "I cannot find her."

"Keep looking," I called back. I hit the elevator button again and stepped inside. There was only one way to go from there and that was up.

CHAPTER SIX

When the elevator stopped on the third floor, the ding seemed even louder than before, and when the doors opened, I realized why. Except for the soft buzzing from the overhead lighting, the third floor was completely empty and all of the office doors were closed, with not one employee in sight. I tried the doors and found them all locked. Had the staff been sent home early to get ready for the celebration? Or was something nefarious going on?

I thought about that scene in the elevator, and it occurred to me that someone could have easily forced Santa into the elevator and straight up here without anyone noticing, all because of that *Out of Order* sign on the door.

Suddenly, I heard someone whistling in the distance. As I crept toward the noise I noticed the floor was wet, and when I peeked cautiously around the corner I saw a janitor sweeping wide circles with his mop. He was tall and thin, well into his seventies, wearing an old pair of overalls with a circle of keys hanging from his belt.

He seemed harmless, so I said, "Hello, there," very quietly, trying not to startle him. "I seem to be lost."

He swiveled in my direction, placed the mop handle under his palm, and crossed his other arm over the top. "Seems that way." He pulled his wrinkled cheeks into a smile but his eyes looked fatigued. "Third floor is employees only."

"I'm sorry. I must have hit the wrong button." I made a show of turning to leave but stopped. "By the way, I noticed a blood smear in the elevator, just so you know."

"I'll take care of it," he said and went back to his mopping. "I've been doing a lot of that this morning."

Trying to draw more information from him, I asked, "Did someone tell you about the blood by the first-floor elevator and also by the emergency exit?"

"Yep," the old man said as he kept working. "Already took care of it."

"Someone must have been hurt pretty badly to be walking around dripping blood."

"I don't question it. I just clean it."

"Did someone tell you there was blood up here?"

"Store manager told me," he answered.

"I don't like blood," I said, trying my hardest not to seem suspicious. "Can you tell me where you were cleaning so I don't step in it?"

He paused to give me once over, then pointed down the hallway. "All leading right to that door."

"Did you check inside?"

"Sure did," he said.

I knew I was pushing my luck, but I had to keep trying. "Where does the door lead?"

"That there is Churchill's private bathroom."

"Who else has a key to that room?"

The janitor plopped his mop into his bucket, splashing water onto the floor. "What are you up to, young lady? You're not lost, are you?"

I hadn't wanted to reveal my identity, just in case Reilly came around asking questions, but if I didn't, I wouldn't get any more information out of him. I dug in my purse for a business card. "Here. That's me, Abby Salvare, from the Salvare Detective Agency. I'm trying to help Hailey Churchill find her father. We think something very bad happened to him and we can't get the police to believe us."

"I think they believe it now," he said, "after what they saw in that bathroom."

"Have the police searched this whole area?"

He secured his mop inside his bucket and rolled it past me. "Yep. Come on. I'll walk you back to the elevator."

"What did you see?" I asked as we walked along.

"A whole mess of blood. Looked like someone tried to clean it up. Did a poor job, though."

"How long were the police here?"

The old man scratched his head. "Couldn't have been too long. After I unlocked all the doors for them, I went downstairs to clean up. I come back up here and they were gone."

I entered the elevator and he rolled his mop and bucket in after me. I pushed the down button and the old elevator door glided shut. "Can you think of anyone who might want to hurt Churchill?"

He rubbed his eyes. "The other day I overheard him and the store manager having a pretty heated discussion. She left the room with tears all down her face. I don't see her as the type to hurt anyone, though."

"Would that be Marcille?"

He nodded.

As the elevator doors opened onto the first floor, I thanked him for his honesty and told him to call me if he remembered anything else.

Suddenly, I heard a loud crash and dashed out of the elevator to see a crowd gathering around Santa's Village. I heard shouting coming from inside the crowd and squeezed through for a better view.

A tall, well-groomed young man in his mid-twenties, dressed in jeans and a white hooded sweatshirt had his hands wrapped around the collar of the skinny Santa I'd seen earlier. The beleaguered Santa, his fake white beard and mustache now askew, struggled to hang onto the arms of his chair as the aggressor attempted to drag him away. The large bag of gifts next to Santa's chair had been tipped over and presents were scattered all around.

I wasn't sure if anyone had called the police so I pulled out my phone and dialed 911, giving the dispatch operator the address as the young assailant shouted to the skinny Santa, "You're sitting there handing out presents as though nothing happened. Get out of his chair."

The angry young man pulled Santa from his chair and they fell into the large, two-story Christmas tree, sending ornaments and candy canes crashing onto the floor around them. Santa fell to the ground and the assailant swung toward the onlookers, breathing hard, obviously in distress. "What are you all doing here? Don't you care that the real Santa Claus is gone and this impostor is taking his place? Doesn't it bother *anyone* that Levi Churchill is missing?"

The battered Santa tried to grab him from behind only to have the agitated attacker whip around and punch him in the jaw.

"Nathan! Stop that this minute!" Marcille cried, rushing toward the fighting men. She stepped over the presents scattered on the ground and tried to pull the young man away. She was knocked backward as Nathan's elbow ratcheted back to lay another hard blow on Santa's skinny cheek.

At that moment Sergeant Reilly brushed past me, out of uniform, followed by three tall men wearing winter jackets and jeans. Two of the officers wrestled Nathan to the ground, flipped him on his stomach, and slapped cuffs on his wrists, but not before knocking over one of my poinsettias, cracking the pot and spreading dirt and petals onto the pad of fake snow. Reilly and the third officer stayed with the bruised and beaten Santa, no doubt to get his statement.

I hurried to Marcille's side and knelt to assist her. "Are you okay?"

She groaned and reached her arm to her lower back, her red jacket pulling taught as she moved. "I think I twisted something in my back. Will you help me up?"

As the two officers marched the young offender out of the store, I had Marcille put her arm around my shoulders and then lifted her gently to her feet.

"Thank you. You're very kind," she said with a faltering smile, showing some humility for the first time.

"Are you sure you can stand?"

"I think I may need to sit for a bit. Will you help me to the bench over there?"

With my arm around her waist for support, I walked her around the gathered crowd, carefully avoiding the broken glass ornaments on the floor, and eased her down onto a white bench with red padding. "Do you mind if I ask you a few questions about what just happened?"

"Go ahead." She sounded a little less friendly than before.

"Who's Nathan? You seem to know him."

"He's Levi Churchill's son." She shook her head. "Poor boy."

"That poor boy just assaulted Santa Claus," I said, "and now he's going to jail."

Her tone had turned curt again, her former humility gone. "Don't judge him. You don't know anything about Nathan."

"Then explain him to me."

"It's a long story, Ms. Knight, and I don't have the time to go into it right now. As you can see, the store is in disarray. I need to get Santa's Village back up and running."

"Again, my name is not Ms. Knight. It's —"

"Abby Salvare," Reilly said as he came strolling up. "I should've known. Wherever there's trouble —"

"There's Sergeant Reilly," I finished. "By the way, this is Marcille Shelby, the store manager."

"We've already had the pleasure of meeting," Marcille said as she brushed the dust from her elbows.

Reilly crouched down in front of her. "Do you need an ambulance?"

"No, I'll recover. I'm just feeling a bit sore." Marcille bent at the waist and stretched to the floor. "I may need a few extra days at yoga this week is all."

"How did you get here so fast, Reilly?" I asked. "I just called a few minutes ago."

He stood up and put his hands on his hips. "We have a booth set up by the choir's stage. We'll be handing out hot chocolate during tonight's celebration, just like usual."

"And police badge stickers?" I asked.

He looked down and quickly removed the sticker from his thick black sweater, a blush staining his fair complexion. "Anyway, just so you know, we're right next to your booth. You better get started on that."

Damn! My booth! "Yes, Sarge, I will." I glanced at my watch. It was almost one-thirty and I hadn't even begun to set up the booth. Plus, I still had to meet Marco so we could get to the hospital to talk to Hailey.

"Anyway," he said, "you ladies should be pleased to know that the DA has already ordered the detective bureau to investigate Levi Churchill's disappearance." Reilly gave me a look that begged the question, *now will you leave it alone?*

"Thank you," Marcille said to Reilly. "Now, if there isn't anything else."

"No, ma'am. Nothing else," Reilly said.

"Thank you." She stretched down one last time and an envelope dropped from her inside jacket pocket, settling on the ground between the three of us. Typed neatly across the middle of the envelope were three bold words.

CHURCHILL'S LAST CHRISTMAS

CHAPTER SEVEN

Sergeant Reilly bent down and picked up the envelope from the floor. "What's this?"

"Good question," I said, looking at Marcille. I stood up next to Reilly and faced her. "I saw that very envelope lying on the ground inside Santa's Workshop next to a puddle of blood – which, by the way, she ordered to be cleaned up, including the trail of blood I found leading away from the workshop."

"You took this envelope out of the workshop?" Reilly asked Marcille.

"I most certainly did not," she exclaimed indignantly. "I wasn't allowed inside because your men had taped it off."

"You most certainly did," I said.

"What about the trail of blood?" Reilly asked me.

"I followed it straight to the elevator just as Marcille came strolling out, calm as could be, in the middle of all the commotion earlier. If I'm right about Marcille, she forced Mr. Churchill out of that little shack and up to the third floor. I was just there. I checked, and every single room is locked tight. You need to get your officers upstairs right now and see if Mr. Churchill is being held up there."

"You're wrong," Marcille cried. "The police have already been to the third floor. We unlocked every office, board room, bathroom, and closet for them and then watched as they searched every single one. Now would you please let me get back to work?"

"Reilly, you're holding the proof," I said. "Check the back of the envelope and you'll see half of a bloody fingerprint. I'll bet if you test it —"

Reilly flipped the envelope over and I stopped cold. There was no bloody fingerprint. The envelope was clean and there was a letter inside.

"That envelope proves nothing." Marcille boldly snatched it from Reilly's hands. "I printed out a whole stack of these. The rest should be sitting on Levi Churchill's desk even as we speak. Every single employee is going to receive one by week's end. It's a letter of notice, informing them that Churchill's department store is going to be sold. I just happened to have one with me."

I still wasn't convinced. "Then what's the significance of *Churchill's Last Christmas?* That sounds like a threat to me."

"A threat?" she scoffed. "That was written at Mr. Churchill's request. Christmas is what this department store has come to stand for. It's what Mr. Churchill has always prided himself in. Above all else, he wanted to thank his employees for their service throughout the holidays, and that's all."

Reilly gave me a smoldering glare as he handed the letter back to Marcille. I used the uncomfortable pause to let the significance of that letter sink in — Churchill's department store was going to be sold. It seemed as though someone other than Marcille had seen the letters on Churchill's desk and took one to confront the man as he was putting on his Santa suit.

That piece of information opened up a whole new theory about Santa's disappearance, but it didn't let Marcille off the hook.

"Why is there a sign on the elevator that says *Out of Order?*" I asked her.

"Damn," she said. "That sign needs to come down. I only put it up this morning so no one would see Churchill coming down before he changes. With all the distractions, I completely forgot about it."

"Can you explain why no employees are working on the third floor?" I asked. "That seems a little strange on the busiest shopping day of the year."

"There is never any clerical staff working on Christmas Eve."

She had a quick answer for every question I could throw at her.

"I still think someone is rushing this investigation," I said to Reilly.

"So does Nathan Churchill," Marcille shot back. "Are you going to knock me over, too?"

I rolled my eyes then turned to Reilly. "Don't you think the crime scene was cleaned up a little too quickly? It feels like the detectives aren't taking this seriously or they wouldn't have removed the yellow tape so soon."

"They seem to be doing a fine job," Marcille said as she stood, wincing a little in pain. "Now, if you'll excuse me, I have a business to run." She walked away with a slight hobble.

I leaned in closer to Reilly. "I don't care what she says; I still think she knows more than she's telling you or the detectives."

"You might be right," he said quietly, "but that's why they're called detectives. I'm not going to tell you again. Let them do the detecting."

As Rosa joined me, Reilly spoke up, "That goes for you, too, Rosa. I don't want to see either of you anywhere near this establishment. Do I make myself clear?"

"Like the crystal," Rosa said and grabbed hold of my arm. "Come with me. I have to tell you something."

As we hurried toward the front door I noticed the old janitor standing in front of Santa's Village with his arms draped over his mop, staring gravely at the mess.

Outside the building, we crossed the street onto the town square and stopped by Santa's sleigh, all set up and waiting for him to arrive that evening. Behind the sleigh were men on tall ladders placing the large golden star on top of the towering Christmas tree. Glancing around to be sure we weren't being overheard, Rosa said, "Churchill's son was taken away in handcuffs."

"I know. I saw him get into a fistfight with Santa Claus. He was shouting at the crowd to go home, clearly upset by the fact that everyone was acting as nothing had happened. And to be honest, I'm upset, too."

"Have the police stopped looking for Churchill?"

"No, but they sure don't seem to be looking very hard."

We began walking back to Bloomers, passing the New Chapel Police booth and the Salvation Army booth, where boxes for toy donations sat in rows alongside the courthouse. Most of the shops around the square had booths on the lawn, their displays almost set up. And there sat the Bloomers booth. Empty.

"Rosa, can I ask you a huge favor? It's almost one-thirty and Marco and I need to visit Hailey in the hospital. If you could –"

She stopped me. "I will talk to Lottie and Grace. We'll watch the store and set up the booth. You have a Santa to save."

I hugged her. "Thank you, Rosa."

My mom and Jillian were setting out books and waved for us to come over. At the same moment, I saw Marco coming out of Down The Hatch, undoubtedly on his way to Bloomers to collect me. He was wearing a thick, black leather bomber jacket with a light grey scarf and thin gloves, black denim, and black boots, making a very sexy Scrooge.

"Rosa, would you make my apologies to my mom and Jillian? I've got to catch Marco."

I caught his eye as I hurried across Franklin. "Marco," I called, "Would you wait for me in front of the shop with the car warmed-up?"

I tried to make a joke about warming up more than just the car, but he clearly wasn't in the mood. He merely turned around and headed for the public parking lot around the corner. After I'd stopped in to thank Lottie and Grace in advance for setting up the booth, Lottie reminded me about the bouquet for Hailey. I grabbed the bouquet and passed through the parlor to give my dad a quick kiss on the cheek before I left.

The car wasn't fully warmed up but the conversation started sizzling the second I entered. Marco's bad mood had momentarily vanished and Team Salvare was back on the case. The hospital was just a quick trip down the highway, so I tried to fill him in on everything I'd learned as quickly as possible.

"I'm not sure where to begin," I said, "so I guess I'll start with the most relevant information first. Levi Churchill is selling his department store, which gives us a whole new motive for his disappearance. I just hope that doesn't mean the celebration will end as well."

"I'm sorry to hear that, Sunshine. I know how much the event means to you."

I wanted to push the subject further, like how much it could mean to both of us if he would just open up and give it a chance. But I had learned my lesson, so I didn't push. "It really does mean a lot, and not just to me. Wait until sundown and you'll see what I mean. The whole town square will be packed with people."

"I can't wait," he said sarcastically. "Did you find out anything more about Marcille?"

"I did. And I totally embarrassed myself in front of Reilly, too, by accusing her of kidnapping Santa Claus."

Marco glanced at me in surprise. "You accused Marcille? That skinny little woman?"

"Well," I said sheepishly, "remember the envelope I'd seen in the workshop? While I was talking to her and Reilly, it fell out of her pocket – or at least I thought it was the same envelope. It had the same words typed on the front. But as it turned out, the envelope didn't contain a threatening letter. It was a letter advising the employees that the business was going to be sold. And there was no bloody fingerprint on the envelope she had either."

"Then what was she doing with one?" Marco asked.

"Good question. Plus, the crime scene tape had been taken down around the workshop and the store was moving along as though nothing had happened. It strikes me as very strange, almost like someone is trying to cover up Churchill's disappearance.

I spoke with a janitor who Marcille had ordered to clean up all of the blood. He had a large key ring full of different keys. I bet he would have access to Churchill's office. He and Marcille could be working together. I don't have any evidence to back that up, but let's just keep it in mind."

"Let's hope Hailey has had enough time to calm down and think. Maybe she can help us out."

"Speaking of Hailey," I said, "I saw her brother Nathan fighting with a Santa Claus substitute this afternoon, trying to pull him out of his chair, shouting for the crowd to go home. He seemed furious that business was going on as usual. Luckily, Reilly and his men weren't far away and were able to handcuff him and haul him off to jail before he could do serious harm to the poor guy."

"It sounds like we need to have a little talk with Nathan," Marco said, "if Reilly will let us into the jail to see him."

"Don't worry. I have a connection. Remember my dad's old friend, Matron Patty?"

"Good thinking," Marco said as he turned down the long winding lane to the hospital parking lot. "But I think we should also let Reilly know what you've found out."

A police officer was posted outside Hailey's second-floor private room but, fortunately, Marco knew him from his year on the force and was able to convince him to let us in to deliver the bouquet. Inside, however, we found Hailey sound asleep.

"What do we do now?" Marco asked.

"I guess we'll just leave the flowers and try to get back here later." But through the shades against the window, I could see that the sun was already settling lower into the sky, and I began to worry that the big Christmas Eve celebration was going to go on without *the* Santa Claus, the man who'd basically started it all.

Tiptoeing across the room, I cleared some space on the windowsill and set the bouquet down among the other floral arrangements that had begun to arrive. Marco nudged me, and I looked around to see Hailey's eyelids fluttering open.

"Did you find my dad?" Hailey asked immediately. The top of her head was wrapped in bandages which stopped just above her eyebrows. Her blonde hair was pulled back behind her ears and her light brown eyes welled with tears. She clasped her hands together. "Please tell me you did."

"We haven't yet, but we're still investigating."

She looked ready to cry, so I hurried to the other side of her bed, pulled the portable recliner up close, and took her hand in mine. "I know you're frightened, Hailey, but it's early yet. We'll find your father. In the meantime, do you have any family who can stay with you?"

"My aunt is at the house picking up some clothes for me," she said. "My brother was here for a while, but he left and hasn't come back yet."

"Hailey, I hate to be the one to tell you, but your brother might not be back tonight. He got into a fight with someone at your dad's store and the police had to take him away."

"Nathan's in jail?" She couldn't hold back her tears anymore. "I told him not to go back to the store. I knew he'd get into trouble."

"When did you tell him this?" I asked.

"When he came to visit me a little while ago."

"Why did you think he'd get into trouble?" Marco asked, perching at the foot of her bed.

"Because he said he was going to find out who hurt me and make them pay," she cried. "And now he's in jail for it."

"Nathan's going to be okay," I said and stroked her slender arm to comfort her. "The most important thing to focus on right now is finding your dad."

Tears streamed down her cheeks. "I'm afraid he's dead."

"We don't know that," Marco said. "Right now he's just missing."

"I was so mean to him this morning," Hailey cried. "I told him I hated Christmas and I hated him. Now what if he *is* dead and that's the last thing I said to him?" She started sobbing uncontrollably. "I didn't mean it." She hit her fist on the bed. "I didn't mean it!"

Marco immediately rose and walked to the window, keeping his back to us as he stared outside.

"We'll find your dad, Hailey," I said, with one eye on my husband. "We just need you to answer a few questions so we can find him faster. Okay?"

"He can't be dead," she wept, grasping my hand. "I need to tell him I'm sorry."

Marco abruptly walked out of the room without even a glance in my direction. It was so out of the blue, my first instinct was to go after him, but I couldn't leave Hailey. I sat beside her on the bed, gave her a hug, and promised again that we would find her dad if she would calm down and answer a few questions.

Finally, she agreed to hear me out. "Can you describe the woman you saw standing by the workshop door this morning?"

She shook her head. "I didn't get a good look at her. I was too far away."

"But the elevator is right next to the workshop," I said.

She looked down as if she were ashamed. "I didn't go directly upstairs. I stopped into the shoe department to see one of my friends. I only stayed for a few minutes. That's when I saw the woman standing by the workshop. Besides, we're not allowed to use the elevator. I had to take the back stairwell."

"Why can't you use the elevator?" I asked.

She cracked a small smile for the first time. "Dad doesn't like anyone using the elevator until he's fully dressed in his Santa Suit."

Then Marcille had been telling the truth. The *Out of Order* sign was simply put up for Churchill's use. Still, Marcille also knew that no one would be using the elevator, which still left her as a potential suspect in my mind.

I continued questioning Hailey. "Do you remember what you told me this morning? You said the woman by the back door was holding something. Do you remember what she was holding?"

She shook her head and sniffled, "I can't explain it."

"What she was wearing? Any jewelry? Is there anything at all that sticks out in your memory?"

"She was wearing a white coat." She sniffled again, so I walked around to the windows to grab a box of tissues sitting next to her get-well gifts.

"She was holding something odd. It seemed out of place." Hailey sighed in frustration and glanced toward the window. Then she saw something that made her eyes light up. "She was holding one of those." She pointed at the bouquet I had brought for her.

"She was holding a bouquet?" I asked.

"No, one of those." She pointed again at the bouquet.

"The holly?"

"No. Next to it."

The *mistletoe*.

CHAPTER EIGHT

Mrs. Guilford!

All at once, the scene came rushing back into my mind: Mrs. Guilford standing at my register with her white gloves and expensive watch, holding a long strand of mistletoe, right before Churchill went missing. Now I knew what her mission was. She was going to meet Santa Claus for a kiss under the mistletoe. That's why she was in such a hurry. She had to get there before he made his appearance.

I thanked Hailey and promised her that, with her help, we'd find her dad in no time, which seemed to cheer her up. Her aunt arrived then with a bag full of clothing, so I gave Hailey a quick hug and hurried into the hall. I met Marco just exiting the bathroom and looped my arm through his.

"We just got a lead," I said. "Let's hit it!"

Once we were in the car, I asked him why he'd rushed out of the room so fast. He patted his stomach and told me not to ask, so I dropped it, even though I knew that wasn't the reason.

"Tell me about our new lead," he said.

"She was in the shop this morning, a widow by the name of Amelia Guilford, one of the wealthiest women in New Chapel. I'm pretty sure she was having a fling with Churchill."

"Abby, if she was having a fling with him, why would she want him to disappear?"

"I don't know yet, but I'm certain she's the key to figuring this whole thing out."

"Let's go talk to her. Do you know where she lives?"

"Nope, but I think I know where she is right now, and I know exactly who can help us find her. Park as close as you can to Bloomers and keep the car running."

He stopped the car in front of my shop and I hopped out. I made a quick stop at the Bloomers booth to find Rosa positioning the pots of poinsettias while Lottie was hanging the holly and mistletoe. I thanked the ladies again for their efforts and assured them I'd be back soon before hurrying over to my mom's booth.

"Jillian," I said, holding my side from running, "don't ask questions, just come with me. I need your help."

My mom started to protest, but I cut her off, "We'll be back in plenty of time, I promise."

"We still have so much to do," Mom called.

"Plenty of time," I called back as I hurried Jillian across the street.

"Woah." Jillian popped into the back of the car and buckled in. "What just happened?"

"We're going to crash a party," I said as Marco pulled out onto the street.

"Oh, a party!" Jillian repeated. "What kind of party?"

"Christmas with the Osbornes."

Jillian immediately unbuckled her belt, ready to jump out of the car. "No way."

"Please, Jill," I said, twisting around to talk to her, "it will only take a few minutes. We just need you to get us inside so I can see if Mrs. Guilford is there. I need to find out what she knows about our missing Santa."

"Amelia Guilford has something to do with Santa's disappearance?"

"I don't want to get into it right now, just trust me on this and don't say a word to anyone about it when we get there."

"My in-laws are *so* not going to be happy with me," Jillian warned. "I told them I had to miss the party to help at your mom's booth."

"When are the Osbornes ever happy with anyone? You probably won't even have to see them. Don't they hire butlers to tend to everything?"

"Don't be ridiculous," she answered. "Just one butler. Abby, really, I don't know about this."

"Come on, Jill. We aren't going to hang around long enough to wine and dine. We're just going there to hunt and gather."

There was silence in the car as my joke fell flat. I looked at Marco then turned to look at Jillian. "It sounded cooler in my head."

After ten minutes of going back and forth with Jillian, Marco turned down the long driveway that led up to the Osborne mansion. Glittering silver icicles dangled from the massive oak trees that lined the drive, while large, brightly lit golden ornaments framed the entrance and portico, and a huge Christmas tree aglow with white lights filled one of the large front windows.

"Fine," Jillian pouted. "One drink and I'm outta there."

"Did you hear what I just said? No drinks. Just get us in."

We were met by a parking valet dressed in a silver suit who offered to park our car, but after taking a look at the festively decorated mansion, Marco informed the valet that he would circle around instead and wait while we went inside.

"Marco," I said quietly, "what happened to Team Salvare? Let the man park the car."

"You don't need me to talk to Mrs. Guilford. Just go."

"Bah, humbug," I said, and got out of the car, slamming the door behind me.

Inside the enormous foyer, Jillian and I were met by a butler dressed in a black suit trimmed in gold who scoffed as we declined to shed our winter gear. He did, however, offer to point us in the direction of the ballroom, to which Jillian replied in the same haughty tone, "I know the way."

The mansion was extravagantly bedecked from floor to ceiling in gold and silver, the paintings on the walls had been trimmed with tinsel, and fragrant, beautifully adorned pine and fir Christmas trees seemed to light up every room and hallway we passed. It did indeed smell like the outdoors, which I found intoxicating, while Jillian made a show of holding her nose.

The party was in full swing when we entered the ballroom. I stared around in awe, overwhelmed by the sheer size of it. A punch bowl the size of a children's wading pool sat at one end of a massive dining table, with row upon row of crystal glassware beside it, and platters of hors d'oeuvres as far as the mouth could water – or rather – the eye could see.

An orchestra at the front of the ballroom played Christmas carols, a fire roared in a ceiling-high stone fireplace along a side wall, and smatterings of people were clustered all around the brightly lit, gilded ballroom. The women were wearing the most expensive clothing I had ever seen and the men were all dressed in black tuxedos.

I looked over at Jillian who was ladling the dark liquid and letting it fall back into the punch bowl. "See," she said with a look of disgust. "Warm wine."

"No time, Jill. Help me find Mrs. Guilford."

After circling the room's perimeter, keeping well out of sight of Jillian's in-laws, we finally spotted Amelia Guilford standing near the fireplace chatting with someone who looked very familiar. As I got closer I realized it was my ex-fiance, Pryce Osborne, the Second.

Pryce and I had been the ultimate mismatch right from the start. He had attended private schools, spent summers in

Italian villas, and not only ate *foie gras* as a child but knew what it was. I had gone to public schools, spent a week every July crowded into a ratty old camper, and thought goose liver spread was something that happened to old geese. But while attending our first semester of law school together, I'd been so taken by the tall, debonair man that I'd ignored our differences and started dating him, eventually becoming engaged to him.

It wasn't until two months before we were to be wedded after I'd received the news that I'd been dropped from law school, that the reality of our differences had hit. Instead of getting a hug from him, I got the cold shoulder – from both Pryce and his parents – and our wedding had been called off soon after. My sole offense had been embarrassing the Osbornes, who considered themselves scions of the community. They hadn't liked me ever since, and I knew neither they nor Pryce would be happy to see me now.

I nudged my cousin. "Pryce is over by the fireplace talking to Mrs. Guilford. Go find a way to distract him. Talk about something he's interested in."

"Like what?"

"Just go! You'll think of something. You married his brother, after all. Talk about stock portfolios or sailing yachts."

"Huh?"

"Just get him to talk about himself. That always worked for me."

Jillian's husband, Claymore, entered the room then, carrying baby Harper dressed in a beautiful white and red Christmas gown. Claymore was accompanied by his parents who clapped for attention and then made an announcement about this being their granddaughter's first Christmas. The crowd gave them the appropriate adulation and then everyone returned to their conversations. A group of photographers lined up in front of the Osbornes and the family began to pose as if they were royalty.

I could see why my cousin was so eager to skip the party. I turned to tell Jillian, only to have her shove her vest at me and take off. I watched in wonder as she made her way over to Pryce, grabbed him by the lapel, and led him away for a family picture, leaving Mrs. Guilford all alone next to the fireplace, a glass of warm wine in her white-gloved hands.

Sometimes Jillian truly amazed me.

When I approached Mrs. Guilford, she cocked her head as if trying to place me.

"Abby Knight Salvare," I said, "from Bloomers Flower Shop."

"Ah, yes. Mrs. Salvare. How good to see you." Her tone indicated otherwise.

"I need to ask you a quick question, Mrs. Guilford."

"Yes, dear, your floral arrangements look lovely. Now if you'll excuse me . . ." She glanced around for someone else to talk to.

"That's not why I'm here, and I didn't do the flowers for this party anyway. I just need to ask you a question about a purchase you made this morning."

I could see the wheels start to spin and then she got a knowing look in her eyes. "I don't have anything to say to you."

I knew I would probably lose her as a customer but I wasn't about to run the risk of Hailey's dad being harmed. "I think you do have something to say, if not to me, then to my friend Sergeant Reilly from the police department."

She glared fiercely. "Ask then."

"You purchased a strand of mistletoe from me this morning, correct?"

There was a burst of applause as the orchestra finished a number. She waited until it had died down before saying snidely, "I'm sure you have copies of your sales receipts. Check for yourself."

"I'm going to take that as a yes. And then you took that mistletoe to Churchill's department store. Is that right?"

"I don't know what you're talking about."

"Don't give me that. I know you went there to meet Levi Churchill for an early morning rendezvous."

Mrs. Guilford lowered her voice, her face turning bright red. "What do you want from me?"

"Answers. I have several witnesses who saw you standing behind Santa's Workshop holding the mistletoe just moments before Levi Churchill went missing."

"Levi's missing?" Her eyes widened and her hand went to her lips. She was noticeably shocked by the news. "For how long?"

"You tell me," I said.

"I *can't* tell you," she replied, lowering her voice, "because I didn't see him this morning."

"I hope you're telling the truth, Mrs. Guilford, otherwise Sergeant Reilly will have to take you down to the station for a little talk."

"Okay, I was there," she ground out, "but I promise you I didn't get to see Levi because someone was in the workshop with him. I could hear them arguing and that's why I left." She glanced around, clearly shaken. "You'll have to excuse me. I need to sit down."

The laughter and music seemed to fade into the background as I watched her make her way to a side chair near the fireplace and slowly sink into it, trembling as she placed her glass of wine on the table nearby.

"I didn't mean to upset you," I said, taking the seat next to her, "but Mr. Churchill may be in serious trouble right now and I'm trying to help him. So please tell me everything you remember."

She let out a shaky sigh. "I bought the mistletoe for Levi so I could hang it above the back door of his workshop. I wanted to surprise him with a kiss before he went on as Santa. It was just supposed to be a way to cheer him up, that's all."

"Why did you need to cheer him up? His daughter Hailey said he was already in a cheerful mood that morning."

"He was cheerful because he loved playing Santa. But he was also dealing with a difficult decision and that's all I can tell you, Mrs. Salvare because I gave Levi my word."

"If it helps, I already know that he's selling his building and hasn't told his employees yet."

Her mouth dropped open in surprise. "How did you find out?"

"I saw a letter to that effect." It wasn't exactly the truth but I still wasn't sure how much I could trust her.

She turned her head toward the crackling fire, wringing her hands together in consternation. "Poor Levi. His business has been failing for some time because of rising internet sales, but he didn't want word to get out to anyone, not even his children, about selling Churchill's until after Christmas so that the celebration could go on as usual. He confided in me because he knew he could trust me. And that's why I went there to cheer him up."

"Could you tell who he was arguing with?"

"Yes." Mrs. Guilford turned her head to look at me. "Even with the carols playing over the speakers and all the chatter from the customers, I could hear his voice as clear as day. He was very angry, angrier than I've ever heard him."

"Who?"

There was fear in her eyes as she answered, "Nathan Churchill. I heard him shouting at his father and got so frightened that I froze."

"Could you hear what Nathan was shouting about?"

"No." She put her head in her hands. "They fight constantly. Ever since his mom died, Nathan hasn't been well."

"If you thought Mr. Churchill was in trouble, why didn't you call for help? There were plenty of people around."

"You don't know Nathan Churchill, Mrs. Salvare. I was afraid of what he might do if he saw me. In fact, I was so afraid that I hid the mistletoe under my coat in case he came out. I didn't want to make things worse."

"I talked to his sister a little while ago and she didn't mention anything about Nathan having problems."

"All I know," Mrs. Guilford said, "is that Levi warned me several times to keep my distance from him. Nathan is the reason we've had to keep our relationship a secret. If Levi is missing, then you'd better believe Nathan had something to do with it."

"If it makes you feel any better, Nathan was arrested this afternoon for assault at the department store," I told her. "So unless he was already released on bond, which I doubt, he should still be there."

"Good. That's where he belongs." She squeezed my hands. "I'm sorry I was rude to you earlier. Is there anything else I can do to help?"

"Yes. Go to the police station and tell them what you overheard at the workshop because they're not taking this matter as seriously as they should be."

"I will," she said. "In fact, I'll do that as soon as I can slip away."

As I got up to leave, Mrs. Guilford said, "One more thing, Mrs. Salvare. Nathan is a very disturbed young man. If he does get out of jail, don't underestimate him."

CHAPTER NINE

The photography session had barely ended when Jillian showed up at my side to retrieve her vest. "There," she said. "I solved your problem *and* got to hold my baby in the family Christmas photograph." She straightened her snowy white vest and smoothed back her long fall of copper-colored hair. "Now let's get out of here before Harper realizes I'm gone and starts to cry."

We slipped quietly away and met up with Marco waiting in the car. Jillian sat in the back looking at herself through the camera on her phone as we drove around the long circular driveway leading us back to the main road.

As we headed to town I filled Marco in on what I'd learned from Mrs. Guilford. "Nathan must have waited until Hailey left the workshop before he slipped inside to confront his dad. That was when Mrs. Guilford arrived for a kiss under the mistletoe. Hailey saw her by the door just before she went up the back stairwell to get the candy canes."

"Did Mrs. Guilford hear what the fight was about?" Marco asked.

"She could hear them fighting, but didn't stay long enough to hear what the argument was about. With the empty envelope inside the workshop, we can assume it was over the sale of the department store."

Marco agreed. "Maybe Nathan wasn't happy when he accidentally found out from a letter and not his own dad."

"Then there was a struggle," I continued, "with one of them hurt badly enough to leave blood behind."

"And the envelope fell to the floor without Nathan realizing it."

"Right. Then Nathan forced his dad up to the third floor knowing it would be empty because of the holiday. When I spoke to the janitor he said there was a mess of blood in Churchill's private bathroom. We know he was up on that third floor. I am positive Churchill is still in that building somewhere."

"But why take him upstairs?" Marco asked. "The emergency exit would have opened onto the alley and from there he could've taken him anywhere."

"Yes, but the emergency exit has an alarm on it. Everyone would have heard it."

"How do you know the alarm hasn't been deactivated?" Marco asked.

"It's just a feeling. But there is one way to find out for sure," I said, giving Marco a devilish grin.

He lifted an eyebrow in interest. "How's that?"

"All we need to do is get in there and push open the door. If the alarm sounds, we know Churchill is still in the building."

Marco gave me his most disapproving glare. "That does not sound like the best plan right now."

"Then we have to get over to the station and question Nathan right now."

"No, Sunshine, we need to find Reilly. I think we should work with him, not against him."

"Then you're going to have to talk to Reilly alone. He isn't very happy with me at the moment."

"I'm not either," Jillian interrupted from the backseat. "The celebration starts in like two hours and I was supposed to help your mom set up her booth. I'm not even in my costume yet."

"Don't worry, Jill," I said, as Marco stopped in front of Bloomers. "You did a good thing today and now you can go change into your costume."

Jillian immediately hopped out and dashed across the street to meet my mom at her booth.

"I'm going to go see if Reilly is still at the police booth," Marco said. "I know he was there earlier. I'll explain our theory and see what he says. Just promise me you won't do anything until I return."

I looked down at the clock on his dash. "We're running out of time."

"Promise me," he said again.

I let my hand drop in my lap. "I promise."

Before I exited the car, Marco leaned over to hug me and whispered in my ear, "When was the last time Team Salvare failed a mission?"

"Never," I whispered back.

Back inside Bloomers, I used some of my nervous energy to close down the shop. It was almost four o'clock and there were no customers. Rosa had left to take Lottie a cup of coffee outside. Most of the town had gone home to get ready for the night's activities. The stores bordering the square were closing down, too, and the employees had mostly finished setting up their booths on the courthouse lawn. Soon the sun would be setting, the festive lights on the lampposts would turn on, and the square would be filled with people once again. This was the calm before the storm.

The clock seemed to tick at double speed as I waited for Marco to return. After closing the register and turning out the lights, I sat in the back at my workbench and pulled out my cell phone. No missed calls. The scent of flowers and the hum of the refrigeration unit usually calmed me after a stressful day, but I had a feeling this day was long from over.

I phoned my neighbor, Theda, who watched our pets while Marco and I were at work and informed her of our situation. She was more than happy to host them at her house for the evening since she wouldn't be joining us for the event. I visited with my dad and Grace who were seated in the coffee-and-tea parlor sipping coffee and watching the small TV screen.

"Join us, won't you, love?" Grace asked, moving toward the coffee bar. "Looks like you could use something to drink. We've switched to decaf, but I'll put a fresh pot on for you."

When the coffee was ready, I sat down with them to discuss what I'd learned about the missing Santa, hoping that their take on the situation would help calm my nerves. "I just don't think the police will handle this quickly enough to find Churchill before the celebration tonight," I told them. "Nathan knows where his dad is. I need to question him, but Reilly has repeatedly told me to stay away from this case."

"How long has it been since Marco said he was going to talk to Reilly?" My dad asked.

"About twenty minutes, but I have a feeling even Marco won't be able to convince Reilly to help."

"Then do it without his help," Dad said.

I gave him a perplexed glance. "I'm sorry. Did I just hear my dad, former police sergeant Jeffery Knight, advise me to defy a direct order from law enforcement?"

He reached over to tweak my arm. "How many cases have you and Marco solved together?"

"Nineteen and counting."

"And how many times have I advised you to stop and let the police handle it?"

I smiled. "Every single time."

"Abracadabra, listen to me," he said. "We both know the New Chapel police are competent, hard-working men and women, but it's Christmas Eve and the whole town is geared up for the celebration, including the police." He tapped the sticker attached to the pocket of his light blue button-down shirt. "Even Reilly is walking around handing out badge stickers, for heaven's sake."

"I know that Dad, but what can I do about Reilly? He warned me to stay away, and he and Marco are buddies."

"When has that ever stopped you?"

Just then Marco knocked on the front door. I let him in and left it unlocked so Rosa and the others could get back inside to freshen up before the celebration officially began.

"Bad news," Marco said. "Reilly won't get us into the jail to talk to Nathan."

"I was afraid of that," I said.

"We had quite a heated discussion over it. But to Reilly's credit, he did tell me that the detectives have uncovered several suspects who had the means, motives, and opportunity to harm Churchill."

"Please tell me Nathan is one of those suspects," I said.

"He is, but Reilly told me that Nathan used his one phone call to contact his family's attorney in Chicago, and the attorney is on his way to see Nathan right now."

"You're right," I said. "That is bad news."

"And that's not the end of it," Marco continued. "Now I'm banned from the investigation as well. He said to stay away or we'd be charged with interfering with police business. He says he's doing this for our protection as well as the police department's."

Jillian burst through the front door, causing the bells to jingle once again, followed by Lottie, Rosa, and my mom, who rushed right up to Marco for the details. Apparently, he had made quite a scene. Before Marco had a chance to explain, we heard singing coming from outside.

We all gathered by the big bay window, Grace wheeling my dad in between us for a better view, as the New Chapel Methodist Choir entered the square singing, *Oh, Come All Ye Faithful*. They were dressed in nineteenth-century clothing, holding thick, black binders and carrying white lanterns that would soon be aglow with candlelight. Their voices filled the surrounding streets with joyous music as they circled the square.

My heart swelled at the sight. I reached over to squeeze Marco's hand, but he'd slipped away. I turned to see him standing all alone at the back of the store, putting on his coat and scarf as though getting ready to leave. A feeling of sadness swept over me. What was keeping my husband's heart so locked up that he couldn't even stand to watch the carolers singing hymns of joy?

I turned toward the window wiping away the tears in my eyes before my family could notice them. But watching the growing crowd outside brought on another depressing thought. Our beautiful celebration would go on even as Churchill lay locked up somewhere, no doubt hurt and possibly dying. No matter what the repercussions were, I simply couldn't let that happen. I had promised Hailey that I would find her dad and I intended to keep it, with or without my husband's help.

At that moment I felt a tap on my shoulder and turned to see Marco motioning for me to follow him to the back. "I have an idea," he said quietly. "With the help of your friend Patty, this would be the perfect time to question Nathan at the police station. But we need to leave right now before his lawyer gets there."

"Let's go," I said.

"Remember," he added, "we'll have to be careful and stay out of sight. Reilly made it very clear what will happen if he catches us. Are you in?"

I squeezed his hands and gave him my brightest Irish smile. "I'm all in."

CHAPTER TEN

I grabbed my coat and purse and we slipped out the back door, walking briskly down the alley to the police station several blocks east of the courthouse. The side streets were beginning to fill in with parked cars and enough people were walking toward the square that we didn't have to worry about being spotted by Reilly. We did have to come up with a plan to talk to Nathan, however.

"Do we go in guns blazing, or do we play it cool?" I asked.

"I don't think we have time to play it cool," Marco answered. "You know the details better than I do so I'm going to let you do most of the talking."

"I say we rattle his cage a bit, get him worked up."

"Go for it, Sunshine. One way or another we need Churchill's location. I don't care how we have to get it."

We rounded the back entrance to the police station when I noticed through the buildings that the sun was just about to set. The clock was ticking down as the time for the Christmas tree lighting ceremony quickly approached.

After entering the building and having our ID's checked, we were searched and then buzzed inside, using Patty's name to get us through.

"We just need ten minutes," I explained to Patty. "I have some new information—"

"I don't want to know," Patty said, cutting me off with a stern look. "I could get in a lot of trouble for this, so make it a quick ten minutes." With that, she showed us to a small conference room just off the main holding cell where Nathan was being kept until his arraignment.

He came into the room in handcuffs, all six feet of him. His brown hair was thick, tapered, and neatly parted at the side. His pale skin was emphasized by the bright light bulb hanging over our heads. Dressed in a thick, white hooded sweatshirt, dark jeans, and expensive sneakers, he stopped immediately and refused to sit down, glaring at us with suspicion. "You're not my lawyer," he said calmly. "What do you want?"

"We want to find your father," I said.

Nathan's body language changed immediately. He pulled out a chair across from us at a gray metal table and placed his cuffed hands on top, one hand thickly bandaged around his wrist. He lifted his chin and cocked his head, looking more intrigued than intimidated. "Could you repeat that, please?"

I was a little thrown by his question. "We're looking for your father."

"Who are you?" he asked, suddenly showing interest.

"I'm Abby and this is my husband, Marco." I didn't reveal anything else. I wanted to hear what he had to say first.

He looked at Marco and then back at me, as though calculating something in his head. "Are you cops? Or are you…?" He paused, waiting for me to fill in the blanks.

We didn't have time to play twenty questions, but I couldn't get a handle on what Nathan was up to. He wasn't behaving irrationally nor was he acting suspiciously. He seemed more confused than anything, so I decided to tell him the truth, or at least part of it.

"I'm a florist and my husband owns a bar."

"Down The Hatch," Nathan said to Marco. "I thought you looked familiar."

Sitting with his arms crossed in front of him, studying the young man intently, Marco gave a firm nod.

"Great," Nathan said. "Now we're getting somewhere. I've already spoken with the police and I'm pretty sure I should be out of here soon." He looked around the room. "Do you guys know what time it is? I still have to get ready."

"Ready for what?" I asked.

"For tonight," he responded emphatically. "As you said, Santa took off, and now I'll have to take over. I would hate for all those people to miss the big show."

I made a mental note of his last few words before I responded. "I didn't say Santa took off. I said we were looking for your father."

"Yeah, well, good luck finding him," Nathan said sarcastically. "The police couldn't even do that."

"Do you know where he is?" I finally asked.

"Who knows? And honestly, who cares? If he wants to disappear on Christmas Eve, then good riddance." Nathan shook his head dramatically. "I guess he wasn't such a great guy after all. It's a shame, really. Everyone thinks so highly of him." He sat back with a satisfied look on his face, completely convinced that we were buying his performance.

I had heard enough. "Nathan, where is your father?"

His demeanor changed drastically. His breathing became staggered and his nostrils flared, but he tried desperately to keep his composure. He shook his head as if to erase his thoughts and continued cheerfully, "I was worried, being locked up here, that everything was going to fall apart. This town needs a Santa Claus and I'm determined to make sure they get one."

"Nathan," I said, mentally wrapping my fingers around his cage, preparing to rattle.

"Are you two coming tonight?" he asked. "I'd love to see the looks on your faces when that star lights up. It will truly be a Christmas celebration you will never forget."

"Nathan," I said again, this time rattling with more authority, "where is your father?"

Like a volcano, Nathan finally erupted. His eyes bulged and his face grew red with rage. He didn't shout but his words came out scalding hot. "Why do you care where he is?"

Now I could see why Mrs. Guilford was afraid of him. In a calm voice, I said, "Because I promised your sister I'd find him."

"No," Nathan said, shaking his head. "That's not true. Tell me why you *really* want to find him. Tell me the truth."

"That is the truth," I said.

"Just say it," he demanded through gritted teeth. "I want to hear you say it."

Marco eased his arm across my lap, ready to push me out of the way if Nathan came at us.

"What do you want me to say?" I asked.

"That you want to save *Christmas*. That's what you're after. You're not looking for my dad. You don't even know him. You're trying to find Santa Claus. You're trying to save your own Christmas. *Say it!*"

I stared at him, unable to respond because he'd hit closer to the truth than I'd wanted to admit. At my silence, Nathan's eyes filled with tears. "That's what I thought."

Marco must have known I was rattled. He reached over and held my hand under the table. What could I say? That, yes, I wanted to find his father and bring the person who had harmed him to justice? And yes, I wanted to tell Hailey that her father was alive and well?

But Nathan was right. What I wanted more than anything was to save Christmas, not just for me, but for the whole town - and even more than that - I wanted to do it for my husband. I wanted Marco to experience the magic I'd felt every year when the star on top of that giant tree lit up, and the whole town cheered. I wanted the distance between us to close. I'd thought that if Team Salvare could solve this case, we'd have a reason to celebrate Christmas together.

"What about *my* Christmas?" Nathan suddenly cried out, a single tear rolling down his cheek. "I want Christmas more than anyone. Do you think you're the only one looking for my father? I've been searching for years. I don't have a father anymore. I'm the victim here and no one is trying to save *me*."

"How can we save you?" I asked.

"Stop looking for Levi Churchill," he demanded. "Let the town see what kind of person he really is, abandoning his role as dear old Santa on Christmas Eve. Forget about him. Let me take over. That's how you can save me."

"We can't do that, Nathan. You know the police will keep looking for him, and once word gets out, this whole town will be looking for him."

"Of course, they will. Everyone loves jolly old Saint Churchill." He began to laugh, his eyes still brimming with tears. "This town doesn't even know the real man. On the outside, he might seem like a warm, caring Santa, but on the inside, he's a cold, heartless bastard."

I think it's time you stop feeling sorry for yourself," I said.

"No," he responded. His breathing slowed. He wiped his eyes and sharpened them on me. "I think it's time you see what Santa Claus looks like...on the inside."

Then Nathan's gaze drifted away and he smiled to himself, humming a cheerful Christmas tune. He seemed suddenly content, so at peace that it frightened me. I glanced at Marco for help, but he merely sat there, silently observing the young man with a distant look in his own eyes. I had no choice but to continue without him.

"I understand your frustration with your father," I said, "but that sounded like a threat. Are you planning to harm him?"

Nathan stopped humming and gave me a cold glare. "You can't possibly understand my frustration."

At that, Marco put his hand on my shoulder. "He's right, Abby. You don't understand." He gave the back of my shoulder a light squeeze, which usually meant to follow along with what he said. Marco was an expert at reading people. I trusted his judgment, so I sat back and let him take over.

Marco put his elbows on the table and continued, "It sounds like your father is a bad guy. I can see why you're upset with him."

Nathan pursed his lips and shook his head. "You don't get it either," he said. "It doesn't matter what I think anymore. This town doesn't see him as a bad guy, but they should. Maybe after tonight, they will."

Marco tried to reason with him. "I see your point, but you can't hurt him. That makes you the bad guy."

"If you had a father like mine," Nathan leaned in, "you'd want to hurt him, too."

Marco leaned in even closer and stared straight into Nathan's eyes. "I did have a father like yours."

I looked at Marco in shock, and so did Nathan. His gaze shifted between Marco and me, as though he was confused, then he sat back in his chair and folded his arms, a smug look on his pale face. "What is this, good cop, bad florist?"

"Hey," I fired back. "I'm an excellent florist."

Marco put his hand on my shoulder again and leaned close to say, "Let me talk to him."

"Talk away," I said.

"In private," Marco added.

I stared at him for a moment, dumbfounded. We were within spitting distance of our prime suspect, who had just clearly stated his intentions to harm his father, and Marco was asking me to step away?

"Trust me," Marco said finally.

I pushed myself from the table and stood. I was buzzed out and ended up on a wooden bench in a hallway just beyond the central office. I sat down, thoughts swirling inside my head like snowflakes in a windstorm. And just like those snowflakes, each thought was unique, making them hard to collect. I rubbed my eyes, trying to make sense of it all.

Was Marco serious about his father or was he using that as an excuse to get closer to Nathan? How would I know? Marco refused to talk about his father.

I checked my watch. The sun was about to set, the celebration would begin soon, and we were no closer to finding Santa Claus than we were before we'd arrived at the station.

As I stood up to stretch my legs, I saw a thin, silver-haired man in a navy pin-stripe suit walking up the long hall toward me. Beside him was Sergeant Reilly.

My heart dropped into my stomach as our gazes locked. I had known Sergeant Sean Reilly for a very long time and he had never before given me such a disappointed look.

CHAPTER ELEVEN

My first instinct was to hide, as foolish as that sounded, but I quickly realized that even if I could have squeezed in behind the water cooler, Marco was still in the conference room with Nathan. I couldn't very well abandon him. So I clasped my hands together and took a deep breath as the men approached me.

Surprisingly, Reilly was being dressed down by the man in the suit, who was saying, "Sergeant, you should know better than to have my client interviewed before I arrive, not to mention his being interviewed by a private detective. I could have your badge for that."

Now I understood the reason for Reilly's look. That man was the Churchill family lawyer, and because of us, Reilly could be in serious trouble. The door buzzed and Matron Patty let them into the room with Nathan, passing by me without a word.

Several long, agonizing minutes passed before Marco finally stepped out. I grabbed his hand, expecting him to usher me out of the building. But instead, he kept a tight hold and said, "Stay here, Sunshine."

The door opened again and to my complete surprise out walked Nathan Churchill followed by his attorney. Reilly came out last, stone-faced and tense.

The lawyer stopped in front of us to say, "I have already informed Sergeant Reilly, and now I'm telling you. If either of you come anywhere near my client or Churchill's department store, I will come after you. I'll file so many charges against you that your heads will spin." And with that, he strutted away.

Humming the same Christmas song as he had earlier, Nathan gave me a secretive smile as he passed by, then began singing the lyrics as he followed his attorney down the hallway. *"Up on the rooftop reindeer pause. Out jumps good ole Santa Claus..."*

The tune echoed softly throughout the corridor as Reilly pointed toward the conference room. "Inside. Both of you. We're going to have a little chat."

"Let me explain," I blurted, as I pulled out a chair and sat down. "I was the one doing most of the questioning, not Marco. He was only trying to calm Nathan down."

Marco put his arm around my shoulders and gave me a reassuring squeeze. "It's okay, Sunshine. You don't need to protect me. I've already told Sean that we were both talking to Nathan."

"Against my orders to stay out of it," Reilly snapped.

"I'm telling you, Reilly," I said, "Nathan knows where his dad is. I can feel it in my gut. Please don't release him yet. Please."

"I'm sorry, Abby," Reilly said, "but we don't have enough evidence to hold him, and anyway, I'm not going to risk my badge because of your gut feeling."

"But Mrs. Guilford even heard Nathan fighting with Churchill moments before he disappeared."

"And in fact," Reilly said, "she's giving her statement to the detectives right now, but it's still not enough to hold Nathan. He'll be released on bond soon. Now calm down and go enjoy the celebration. We'll find Churchill. It'll just take some time."

"What kind of time?" I shot back. "Days? Weeks? Nathan has something planned for *tonight*, Reilly. He basically told us so."

Reilly folded his arms across his thick black sweater. "Okay, what's he planning?"

I turned to Marco, hoping that maybe he had extracted at least one clue after I'd left, but Marco said, "He wouldn't tell us, Sean, but I agree with Abby. The clock is ticking and your detectives need all the help they can get. We're already involved. Why not let us help?"

"You heard the attorney's threat," Reilly said. "Now I'm telling you for the last time, *stay out of it,* because he isn't kidding. He'll come after you with everything he's got. The only thing I can do for you right now is to make sure you don't get yourselves into any more trouble, so if I see either of you snooping around Churchill's this evening, you'll have to deal with me first."

The air was growing colder and the first few flakes of snow came tumbling out of the sky as Marco and I walked back to the town square. We passed groups of families on their way to the courthouse lawn, bundled up and laughing together. The electrified decorations illuminated the storefronts and the lamp posts came on as darkness settled around us. The Christmas Eve celebration on New Chapel's town square had always been one of my most beloved memories, but as we walked back in silence, I couldn't help but wonder if this would be the last one.

Despite its deserted décor, Down The Hatch was bursting at the seams with revelers, which wasn't surprising.

Being one of the only establishments on the square still open before the celebration began, Marco's bar didn't need any help attracting customers.

He let go of my hand and gave me a quick peck on the cheek.

"Is this the first time Team Salvare fails our mission?" I asked. "On Christmas Eve?"

He wrapped his arms around me, blocking a brisk burst of flurries swirling down the sidewalk. "I don't know what else to do."

"Well, I do. We need to locate Nathan and track his movements so I can keep my promise to Hailey."

"Sweetheart, I want to find Churchill as badly as you do, but I think we need to trust Reilly with this one. I don't want to have my private investigator's license revoked, or worse, both of us end up being sued."

"I don't care what you or Reilly or even Nathan's fancy attorney says, there has to be a way to save Churchill without any of that happening. I'm not going to let Hailey or the town down. So with or without you, I'm going to find Nathan."

Marco gazed down at me and sighed. "There's no way I'm going to talk you out of this, is there?"

"Nope."

He thought it over for a moment then said, "I'll go check in with Rafe to make sure he's not overwhelmed at the bar, then I'll meet you at Bloomers to figure out our next move."

I rested my cheek against his coat and gave him a fierce hug. "Thank you, Marco." Then, while still in his arms I dared to ask, "Will you tell me what you said to Nathan about your father?"

He held me at arms-length and gave me his sexy, dismissive smile I knew all too well. "Let's focus on our next move first." He kissed me and left me there wondering.

I turned around to see Mom and Jillian just leaving their booth, their arms loaded with empty boxes and extra decorations as they headed across the street toward Bloomers. I unlocked the front door for them and we were immediately announced by the jingling bells. We were reunited with Lottie and Rosa, who were warming up in the candlelit tea parlor with my dad and Grace.

Most of the lights in Bloomers were off, leaving only the soft light streaming in from the big bay window facing the square. This would normally have been my favorite part of the evening: the booths outside were all set up, the trees surrounding the courthouse glowed with colored lights, the carolers were singing, their voices carrying around the square, and even the snow had made its fateful first appearance.

At any moment the big bell in the courthouse steeple would ring out to signal Santa's arrival to his sleigh. The booths would open and the celebration would begin. Then, at six o'clock, Santa would stand and count down the lighting of the star on top of the tree. But it wouldn't be Churchill out in that sleigh. It would be Nathan. I felt detached from it all, worried about our missing Santa, and saddened by my husband's secret burden.

"After you and Marco left," Dad said, "I filled everyone in on your plan to question Nathan. How did it go?"

"Not good," I answered, dropping into a chair in the candle-lit parlor. "We didn't have enough time to get any real information before his lawyer showed up and got him bonded out."

"Do you still think he kidnapped his father?" Lottie asked.

"More than ever," I answered. "Nathan wouldn't admit to anything, but I could tell by his behavior that he has something bad planned for his dad tonight." I looked at the gang seated across from me, giving me sympathetic stares, and sighed. "I just can't put the pieces together."

"How can you be sure?" Rosa asked.

I watched the single candle flame dance inside the glass bell jar on my table. "I can't explain it. I just know."

Grace finished pouring fresh cups of decaf for my mom and Jillian who had just sat down at the table next to mine. She placed a cup at my elbows and began to pour. "If at first, you don't succeed," she started.

"I've tried, Grace," I said solemnly, "and I've tried again, but I seem to have only made things worse. Now Nathan's lawyer is threatening us with a lawsuit if we go anywhere near Nathan, or even Churchill's store, which means we're banished from half of the courthouse square. On top of that, Reilly said he'll be keeping his eye out for us."

"Maybe the situation's not as bad as you think," my dad said, trying to cheer me up. He pushed away from the table and rolled himself closer to face me. "I can't imagine any son wanting to harm his own father on Christmas Eve."

"You should have seen the look in his eyes," I explained, "the hatred in his voice. He wants his father to suffer. I just wish we had more time. We were so close to making him talk."

"Come on over to the booth with us tonight," Lottie offered. "Hand out some flowers. Make some people happy. Try to enjoy yourself."

"I don't know," I said despondently. "With Churchill missing and Marco hating the holiday, I seriously doubt I'll be able to enjoy myself, especially with Nathan running the show."

My mom lifted herself from her seat and stood behind me. She wrapped her arms around me and gave me a kiss on the cheek. "We don't have to attend the celebration tonight, sweetheart. We can stay here with you."

"Yes," Rosa said and raised her coffee cup. "Who needs the large celebration. We will have Christmas Eve right here at Bloomers."

I patted my mom's arm and looked over at Rosa. "That's very kind of you, but I'll be fine. Go and enjoy yourselves. I'll wait for Marco and see what he wants to do."

Just then the courthouse bell began to ring, echoing throughout the town square.

"That's your cue," I said.

Jillian put down her coffee cup and turned to my mom. "Is it time?"

"It's time." Mom gave me one last kiss on the cheek. "I'll go get our costumes. And Jeffery," she said to my dad, catching him as he quietly wheeled himself back toward the television, "don't get too comfortable."

With my chin in my hands, I watched as my team and family prepared for the night's celebration, buzzing around inside the flower shop with the same excitement that I used to feel.

Lottie pulled out a basket of pruning supplies from behind the counter. "Grab the ribbons, Rosa."

Grace began slipping on an extra pair of mittens. "Don't forget to layer," she announced. "It will be quite chilly out there."

My mom came out of the workroom with three full-length costumes draped over her arms and a large travel bag in her hands. Jillian grabbed the bag and opened it while my mom placed the suits on out on the counter. I joined them.

"Abs, look at all of this stuff!" Jillian said.

"Once I started making the costumes, I just couldn't seem to stop," Mom explained. She pulled out elf slippers and white wigs, a Santa's mustache and beard, and thick bushy white eyebrows. There was also rouge for the cheeks and little round gold glasses for Mrs. Claus.

"Mom, you've outdone yourself this time," I said, as she took out a red hat with a fuzzy white ball on top.

"I did, didn't I?" she replied. "Once we're fully dressed, you won't even recognize us anymore."

A sliver of a smile spread across my face. "Is that so?"

CHAPTER TWELVE

Marco knocked on Bloomers' front door. Fairly dancing with excitement, I let him in, took his hand, and led him straight to the costumes and accessories spread out across the counter. "Marco, I have an idea."

He glanced from the costumes to my mom and Jillian, who were just as clueless as he was. Then he narrowed his eyes at me. "I already don't like it."

"Just hear me out," I said. By that time, Lottie, Grace, and Rosa had grouped around the counter to listen. "We know Nathan is going to be at that celebration at some point, but we aren't allowed to go near him. Right?"

Marco nodded.

"And we're almost certain that Churchill is still somewhere in that building, but we can't get in without the risk of getting caught. Right?"

"He *might* be in the building," Marco cautioned, "but if you think I'm getting into a Santa costume and sneaking into Churchill's department store, you've lost your mind."

"No," I corrected. "We don't sneak in. We blend in. The square is going to be jammed with people, some wearing

Christmas costumes. Reilly will be looking for Abby and Marco, not Santa and Mrs. Claus."

"Or their cute helper elf!" Jillian exclaimed.

"I'm not keen on the idea of dressing up as Santa Claus," Marco said stubbornly.

"Just listen," I said. "Nathan wants to take over for his father, which means he could be sitting out in that sleigh right now."

"Then I will go check," Rosa announced, tossing the end of her scarf over her shoulder. "No one will be looking for me." Before I could stop her, she left the shop and hurried across the street.

"It's still too risky," Marco said. "You heard what Reilly told us. We have to take him seriously."

"I know, Marco, but I wouldn't be able to live with myself if something happened to Churchill tonight and we did nothing to save him. Would you?"

"Excuse me," Mom interjected. "If I'm understanding this correctly, your whole idea revolves around using the costumes I've spent hours crafting in my spare time."

That stopped me. I hadn't even considered that my plan was not only risky but incredibly selfish, too. "I'm sorry, Mom. You're right. These costumes are your creation and you should use them as they were intended, to run your booth."

"You didn't let me finish," Mom said. "Do you realize that this is the first art project I've ever made that you have been truly excited about?" She held out her arms and I stepped into them. "It's my Christmas miracle," she whispered in my ear as she hugged me. Stepping back with tears in her eyes she said, "I'm happy to let you use them. Go find our missing Santa."

But Marco continued to play devil's advocate. "Let's say we do get out there unnoticed and find a spot to stake out Nathan. What then?"

"We keep an eye on him," I answered honestly. "At six o'clock he's going to be sitting in the sleigh, counting down the lighting of the tree. I guarantee it. That's what he wanted us to see, so that's where we need to be. If Nathan does anything suspicious, we'll alert Reilly."

Marco shook his head. "I'm not dressing up as Santa Claus," he said finally.

"Fine," I fired back. "Then I'll spend Christmas Eve without you. Just like last year."

My dad wheeled himself out of the parlor and stopped his chair in front of both of us. "You don't have to decorate your business," he said to Marco. "You don't have to show football on the television." He reached behind him and pulled out the fluffy pillow he used for back support. "But you're putting on that costume and accompanying my daughter to the celebration." He threw the pillow into Marco's arms. "So you might as well look the part."

Holding the pillow, Marco said, "I'm not going to leave your daughter alone. I'm just saying there has to be a better way of getting close to Nathan."

"Then think of one," my dad said.

I could tell my husband was racking his brain, looking around the room as if something might trigger an idea. Finally, his eyes came to rest on the costumes. He breathed in deeply and blew it out, as he always did when he didn't want to do something.

"We have to try, Marco," I said softly.

He let out a sharp sigh. "Let's get this over with."

Lottie and Grace wished us luck and left for the Bloomers booth. My mom and dad bundled up and headed for the door, but before my mom could wheel him out, my dad stopped to say, "I'll try to keep Reilly occupied. Have your phone near you with the volume turned up. I'll let you know if he leaves the police booth."

I thanked my parents again and locked up the door behind them. Outside, the courthouse lawn was swarming with people, and I was beginning to feel thrills of excitement race up my spine. I turned to see Marco holding up the thick black boots we had pulled from my mom's travel bag. Jillian had already taken off to change in the bathroom, which left Marco and me all alone. I tried to thank him, but he stopped me.

"You don't have to thank me," he said as he began to pull his suit on over his clothes.

"But I *want* to thank you. I know you think this is a bad plan."

"Not true," he said and fastened the large buckle around his trim waist. "I think it's risky and I'm not thrilled with it, but I don't think it's a bad plan. It's our only plan."

Wearing my warm woolen sweater and a turtleneck beneath the Mrs. Claus outfit for warmth, I donned the red leggings and matching long red velvet coat. "I know you hate Christmas," I said, zipping up the front of the coat, "yet here I am dragging you into the middle of the celebration, even after our fight. So just let me say thank you."

Marco turned around to look at me. "Sweetheart, I'm sorry about today in the car. I shouldn't have snapped at you. This is a difficult time of the year for me, but I don't hate Christmas. It's just not easy for me to talk about, that's all."

I wanted to ask him more, but it wasn't the right time. "I'm sorry about what my dad said to you. He's very adamant about traditions, especially Christmas."

"And football," Marco added. He pushed the pillow into his suit around his mid-section and shifted the black belt around his stomach. He looped the straps of his bushy white beard around his ears and positioned the fluffy whiskers to cover his lips, chin, and neck.

I handed him the finishing touch, a floppy red hat with a thick black buckle in front, and a fluffy white ball attached to the top. I fixed the ball so it draped appropriately to the side and had to chuckle to myself.

He gave me a surly expression. "How do I look?"

I smiled. "Like Santa Claus." I tied the straps of my red and white bonnet under my chin then hooked the gold-rimmed glasses around my ears, positioning them down the bridge of my nose. "How do *I* look?"

A grin lifted one corner of Marco's white mustache. "Like my wife."

Jillian stepped through the curtain and twirled before us, her elf shoes jingling. "I told you I could rock this skirt. I'm not sure about the tights, though."

After looking Jillian over, I realized that she was wearing the outfit my mom had made for me. Thank goodness for the tights, because the skirt was way too short for her long legs. She was decked out in green and black, with her tights a swirling mixture of the two. Her vest was a little loose, but the skinny green hat and elf ears made up for it. I had to admit that she did look cute.

Rosa returned with bad news. "I couldn't find Nathan anywhere. He is not in the sleigh. There are hundreds of people out there. Finding him would be like looking for a needle in a matchbox."

"You mean haystack," said Jillian, the one who rarely got her own words right.

"It's almost time for the tree lighting," I said, looking at my watch. "Thirty minutes, to be exact. Where could Nathan be?"

"I went into the department store to look, too," Rosa explained, "but it is too busy. The store has not closed early like the other shops and there are still too many last-minute customers."

I glanced at Marco in a panic. "That means he could be anywhere." Turning to Rosa, I said, "Will you help my mom at her booth? My dad will be keeping Reilly occupied and I want you to watch the area for Nathan. If you see him, call me immediately. I'll have my phone with me at all times."

Rosa opened the door, letting in a blast of cold air. "I will keep my eyes out for him like an eagle."

Marco, Jillian, and I stood by the big bay window and gazed out at the sea of people filling the square. I tapped my watch. "It's now or never, Marco."

"Are you giving me the option?" he asked.

"No," I responded. "Now."

We left Bloomers and walked quickly past Down The Hatch, taking the long way around the square. The snow was falling softly and consistently, forming a white glistening glaze on the sidewalks and the glowing branches of the trees. We cut through the crowd, mingling with the many shoppers at booths on the southern side of the courthouse lawn, keeping our distance from the police booth. Jillian stopped momentarily to grab a free glass of hot cider and I ushered her along impatiently. Beyond the courthouse, on the north lawn, we could hear the church choir singing. There was no sign of Nathan.

We rounded the courthouse and I was overwhelmed by the sight in front of me. Churchill's department store was completely lit up, every window wrapped in golden light strands. Parents with their children filled almost every inch of space on the sidewalk, taking pictures with the oversized ornaments and larger than life candy canes along the front of the store.

On the courthouse lawn opposite Churchill's, outlined with a thick red rope, stood a larger version of Santa's Village, even down to his miniature workshop at the back. But instead of Santa's big red and gold chair sitting beside the workshop, a white wooden sleigh trimmed with colorful gold swirls sat there instead, with a path outlined in more red rope leading up to it. Beside the workshop sat the massive, glowing Christmas tree, decorated with at least a mile of multi-colored lights and yards of tinsel.

I gazed up at the top, where the Christmas star, still unlit, swayed in the gentle evening breeze. "Isn't it beautiful?" I asked Marco. I felt an overwhelming sense of happiness, standing there with my arm looped through his, sharing that beautiful sight with him, safely hidden amidst all the people filling the area.

That happy feeling vanished as Marco grabbed Jillian and me and pulled us behind the workshop. "We've been spotted."

CHAPTER THIRTEEN

Marcille came marching around the back of the workshop heading straight for us, carrying her ever-present clipboard and wearing a thick white coat over her festive red dress. She was heavily out of breath, with her perfectly towering hairdo now hanging in strands around her cheeks. When she realized it was us beneath the costumes she gasped. "You're not supposed to be here. I have strict orders from Churchill's attorney to notify him immediately if I see either one of you."

How had she recognized us beneath our costumes? I reached up to check my wig and realized some of my bright red hair had escaped the netting underneath. "Okay, before you rush to judgment, Marcille," I said, hastily tucking in my hair, "let me explain—"

She cut me off. "I don't have time for explanations. You're here, you're in costume, and I need you *now*."

"You don't understand," I said. "

Marcille slid behind the workshop and checked her watch. She got right up in our faces. "This store has been understaffed for weeks. I have been running around in these heels for ten hours. Santa is missing and not one employee will step up and take his place, not after what Nathan did to the last one."

She blew a loose strand of hair from her eye. "There are over one hundred impatient people standing in that line and if one more person asks me where Santa is, I am going to lose my patience! Now," she pointed at Marco, "you get your ass up on that sleigh and take pictures with these people or I dial Churchill's lawyer." She opened the back door to Santa's workshop then pulled out her cell phone. "It's your choice."

Before either of us had a chance to respond, Jillian strode straight inside the workshop and stepped out the front door to an overwhelming cheer. Through the open doors, I could see her twirl in her little skirt and blow kisses to the crowd. Then she looked back inside and motioned for us to join her.

"Please, Marco," I said. "It'll buy us some time so I can keep a lookout for Nathan."

He breathed in deeply and let it out slowly. "Do not leave my side," he demanded.

"I won't." I squeezed his hand. "I promise."

The crowd cheered even louder as Marco made his entrance as Santa Claus. Marcille followed him out and pulled open the rope that was keeping the desperate children back. Jillian was near the front of the line and I positioned myself on the opposite side of the sleigh, close to Marco but with a perfect view of the department store and the surrounding area. Marcille gave us a thumbs up.

Let the show begin.

Marcille gave instructions to Jillian, and my cousin immediately stepped into the role of Santa's helper, almost as if she were born to be an elf. One by one, she helped the children climb up onto Santa's lap while the parents gathered around the sleigh for their photo. Under Jillian's direction, the children exited on my side of the sleigh and were reunited with their parents a few steps away at the photo booth.

Everything was operating so smoothly that I began to worry. Number one on my list was why Nathan hadn't shown up to play Santa, as he'd claimed he was going to do. Only ten minutes remained until the tree lighting ceremony and people had started to exit Churchill's department store in anticipation of it. As the crowd grew, so did the knot in my stomach.

"Hello there, Mrs. Claus," I heard from behind me.

I tore my gaze away from the crowd to see Rhondella Saddler standing beside Santa while her son sat on his lap.

Trying my best to portray a jolly Mrs. Claus, I stepped over to her and said, "Merry Christmas to you, dear."

"Don't give me that crap," she said in a low voice. "I know who you are."

Rhondella had recognized me, too? I reached up and found another strand of red hair had come loose. That and my darned freckles had to be giving me away. I'd have to be more careful or Reilly would be the next one to spot me.

"Listen," Rhondella said, "how about comping me on the photo? It's bad enough I have to wait in line all day for it, I have to pay, too?"

"Take that up with the management," I whispered.

Thomas sat there with his little back as straight as a soldier's, gazing up at Santa with his sweet blue eyes as he listed the presents he wanted to give his older sister and grandparents.

"What about you, Thomas?" Marco asked. "What would you like for Christmas?"

The young boy looked at his mom as though asking for her permission to answer.

"He already received his present," Rhondella said. "Didn't you, Thomas?" She turned to me. "Going on all day about some toy he wants when he already received a perfectly good present this morning. Isn't that right, Thomas?"

He nodded politely.

"Go ahead," Marco said. For the first time, I saw a glimmer of happiness in my husband's eyes. His voice changed slightly. It was deeper and more animated. Whether or not Marco knew it, he was actually embracing the character. "What do you want more than anything in the world? You can tell me. I'm Santa Claus."

The photographer snapped their photo just as Thomas leaned over to whisper something in Marco's ear. Rhondella pasted on a fake smile as one more picture was taken and then before Jillian could step up, she lifted Thomas straight off of Marco's lap and set him on the ground next to her.

I heard the faint ding of my cell phone coming from the pocket of the long red coat, but at that moment Rhondella stopped beside me to sneer, "By the way, I'm not paying for those photographs."

I muttered under my breath as she walked away. Rhondella's behavior had so annoyed me that I turned to Marco to comment on her - only to notice my husband wiping tears from his eyes.

"Abs," Jillian whispered from the other side of the sleigh, but I was too concerned with my husband to pay attention to what she was trying to tell me. I was just about to lean in close to ask Marco what was wrong when Jillian called, "Mrs. Claus!"

I looked immediately to where she was pointing and spotted Nathan Churchill weaving his way through the crowd inside Santa's Village.

"There he is!" I said to Marco, as Nathan hopped over the rope and ran across the street, heading straight for Churchill's. Moving as fast as I could in my long coat, I followed, glancing back long enough to see that Marco wasn't behind me. As Nathan entered the department store's front doors, I paused at the curb to see what was keeping Marco only to discover that he hadn't moved off the sleigh. In fact, he wasn't even looking my way, and neither was Jillian. Then I saw the reason why.

Standing in front of my husband, blocking the group of waiting children, stood an angry Sergeant Reilly, his hands on his hips. "This way. Let's go," he said, motioning to Marco.

I cupped my hands around my mouth and shouted, "Reilly. Stop! You've got to help me." I gestured toward Churchill's. "It's Nathan!"

Then I hiked up the red velvet coat and ran across the street, darting around people still posing for pictures with the giant ornaments and candy canes, and dashed in through Churchill's main entrance. As I raced down the center aisle, dodging the last few shoppers who hadn't made it out yet, I heard the loud ding of the old elevator and made my way toward the back of the store. I knew it was Nathan on his way to the third floor. I could feel it in my gut.

Breathless, I stopped in front of the gold doors to see that the *Out of Order* sign was still posted, yet the lights above the elevator showed it rising slowly upward. Making a quick assessment, I hurried for the back stairwell hoping I could beat Nathan to the third floor. I hoofed it up three flights of stairs and then held myself against the wall until I caught my breath. Quietly, I pushed open the door and peeked into the hallway.

Nothing. No sign of Nathan. No loud ding from the elevator. The overhead lights were off, the Christmas music from below had stopped, and the silence around me was eerie. Was he still on the elevator or had I missed him?

I backed into the stairwell and pulled the door closed with a soft click. I was still feeling light-headed from my mad dash up the stairs, so I took a moment to sit on the steps, catch my breath, and think. Remembering the text message that had come in earlier, I reached inside the red velvet coat and pulled out my phone. I held it up to read the message – a warning from my dad that Reilly was headed our way.

Quickly, I dialed Marco, resting my elbow on the stairs behind me as it rang. I glanced to my right and then it hit me. There were more stairs going up. But I was already on the top floor, which meant the stairs could only lead to the roof.

The rooftop! That's where Levi Churchill was.

Up On The Rooftop was the song Nathan had been humming during our interview at the jail and then again when he and his lawyer had passed me in the hallway.

The pieces started to fall into place. Nathan hated his father. He didn't want us to miss the big show so everyone could see, in his words, what Santa Claus looked like on the inside. Then he'd sung that song, his little joke on us.

Now I knew what his plan was. He was going to push his father off the roof during the tree lighting ceremony. I could imagine the scores of people looking up at the star, counting down the seconds until it was lit, only to witness a tragedy that would change the fate of Christmas in New Chapel forever.

Marco answered the phone and immediately asked where I was, but before I could respond, the third-floor door opened, and there stood Nathan gazing at me in surprise. Before I could move, he lunged at me, causing the phone to drop from my hand. I pulled away from him and raced down the stairwell, my heart pounding against my ribs, my feet not even touching every step, almost collapsing at each landing.

But I couldn't stop because Nathan was right on my heels. He grabbed the bonnet still on my head, causing the strings to pull tightly around my neck before giving way. I made it down to the first floor and out of the stairwell before Nathan finally caught me.

He put his hand around my mouth, and I bit down hard, so hard that he loosened his grip, allowing me to break free. That's when I spotted the emergency exit and the sign, *CAUTION – ALARM WILL SOUND.*

I was almost at the exit when Nathan grabbed me once again, only this time around my neck, squeezing until stars filled my field of vision. Struggling powerfully, I elbowed him hard in the ribs only to have my arm clamped against my side. Somehow, I managed to maneuver us around so I'd be facing the door, only to feel my legs beginning to collapse beneath me. I knew I'd be out cold within seconds, so I used my remaining strength to pull one booted foot up.

The last thing I remember thinking before blacking out was that I'd better be right about that alarm.

CHAPTER FOURTEEN

The first thing I noticed was that the air was cold - so cold my whole body was shivering. I opened my eyes and waited for them to adjust to the darkness before glancing around to see where I was.

Dear God, I was up on the rooftop.

I tried to move but my hands were tied firmly behind my back. Nathan had propped me against the two-foot-high redbrick wall that rimmed the department store's flat, graveled roof, my legs straight out in front of me, my head and neck exposed to the frigid night air. My neck ached from the icy breeze and my ears rang from the blaring alarm I had triggered.

I winced as I turned my head to look over my right shoulder, where I could see the large star on top of the town's Christmas tree glowing brightly. From below came the cheerful crooning of the crowd singing Christmas songs with the choir. The countdown was over. The celebration had officially begun. Had anyone even heard the alarm?

Suddenly, I heard Nathan cry out, "Stay back! Keep them back."

"Calm down. I just want to talk to you," came Marco's reply, the sound of his voice filling my whole body with relief.

I looked to my left and saw Levi Churchill just a yard or so away. He was slumped over, his hands tied behind him, also up against the short wall, but he seemed barely alive.

"I said keep them back or I *swear* I will do it," Nathan shouted, a desperate quiver in his voice. He stepped out of the shadows and stalked toward me, a long, sharp knife in his hand.

Marco stepped out from the shadows then, too. "Nathan, think about what you're doing." He had shed the red suit and was shivering in his black jeans and a long-sleeved t-shirt. He saw that I'd come to and locked eyes with me, his concern for me written all over his face. I gave him a slight nod to let him know I was okay, although on the inside I was anything but, sitting just inches away from a three-story free fall.

Behind him, I could see Reilly standing at the entrance to the stairwell accompanied by several plain-clothed officers with their guns drawn. Marco slowly backed up to them and spoke quietly, but I couldn't hear what he was saying.

Keeping one eye on Marco and the cops, Nathan said to me, "You should have listened to me. This had nothing to do with you. You should have let me take over."

"I couldn't do that," I said. "I wasn't out to get you, Nathan. I just wanted to save your father."

"You wanted to save your own Christmas," he scolded. "So did I."

"Nathan," Marco said, drawing his attention away from me, "listen to me now." He walked slowly toward us with his palms facing forward, showing that he was unarmed. "The police are going to stay back, but only for a few minutes."

As he said it, Reilly and his men stepped back into the stairwell, letting the door close behind them. That left Marco, Levi, and me alone on the roof with Nathan.

"Stay where you are." Nathan held the knife out in front of him. "You can have your wife when I'm done. Just stay back and let me finish what I started." He walked over to

Churchill and pulled his chin up by the beard. "Isn't that what you always say? I never finish what I start?"

Levi Churchill struggled to lift his eyelids. His forehead was swollen and bruised, with dried blood matted in his beard and snow covering his sullied Santa suit and hat. He must have been up on the roof since his disappearance that morning.

"Will you let my wife move away from the edge?" Marco asked. "That's all I want."

"No," Nathan answered. "You don't always get what you want. That's another lesson my father taught me." He bent down closer to his dad, still keeping an eye on Marco. "All I wanted was this store." He put his free hand around Churchill's suit collar and tried to lift him. "Stand up!"

Churchill attempted to stand but fell back down again. Nathan put the knife between his teeth then pulled his dad up so that he was seated on the narrow rim of the roof. Holding onto his father's Santa suit with one hand, he put the knife back in his other and pointed the blade at Marco. "This store has been in our family for three generations, did you know that? He promised I could take it over when he retired. Then just like that, he decided to sell it right out from under me." Nathan inched his father backward, closer to the edge.

"Let me talk to you," Marco said, trying to stop him.

"I just wanted to talk to *him*," Nathan continued. "But my dad never listens. I tried to make him talk this morning but he pushed me away. I cut my hand wide open. I was bleeding everywhere, but he didn't care. He had presents to hand out."

"It doesn't have to end this way," Marco said.

"But it does," Nathan shouted and looked at his father. "He said so himself. This is Churchill's last Christmas."

"Stop, Nathan," Marco demanded. "We were interrupted earlier. I didn't get a chance to finish my story."

"I'm not interested in your story," Nathan snarled. "This is my story and it has nothing to do with you. It's between me and my father now, and there isn't anything you can say to stop me."

"The least you can do is let me finish," Marco said.

Nathan stared down the tip of his blade at my husband, steam escaping into the cold air with each heavy breath. "Why?" he asked. "Why should I care about your story?"

"Because I understand what you're going through," Marco answered honestly. "I know exactly how you feel."

Nathan gave him a scathing glance. "How could you possibly know how I feel?"

"Because my father died on Christmas Eve," Marco said, his words coming out strained and filled with pain. "He died because of me."

Nathan held his father firmly on the edge but paused. I held my breath as Marco took one step closer. And although my husband stood tall and powerful, his face held a look of vulnerability. It was the look he'd tried to hide in the car that morning. It was the look he'd given before leaving Hailey's hospital room.

"You told me you hated your father," Nathan said.

"I *did* hate my father," Marco answered. "I hated him for years."

"Why are you telling me?" Nathan asked. "It's not going to change anything."

"I've never told anyone," Marco admitted. "I've never been able to. If anyone would be able to understand my story it would be you."

Nathan lowered his arm and held the knife at his side. He kept hold of his weakened father. All it would have taken was one push and Churchill would have been gone. "Go ahead," Nathan said. "I'm listening."

"My dad owned a small Italian diner," Marco began. "As soon as I was old enough, he expected me to work with him in the kitchen, every day after school. The diner was busy all the time, and we would stay open on every holiday, even Christmas Eve. He said the hard work would teach me discipline. It would make a man out of me. And I hated him for it."

"Then why do you care if he's dead?" Nathan asked.

"Because my dad didn't do it to hurt me," Marco said. "But at the time I didn't get it. I just wanted to be a normal teenager and have a real Christmas with presents to open under the tree. I didn't want to be slaving over a hot stove."

Marco paused to draw in a breath. "The year I turned fifteen, we got into a huge argument. I wanted to spend Christmas Eve with my friends, and he said no." Marco stopped again to glance at me.

I didn't want him to see me crying but I couldn't move my hands to wipe the tears away.

Slowly he moved another step closer to me, continuing his story for both of us to hear. "My dad tried to get me to stay at the restaurant with him by giving me an early Christmas gift – a football. He even offered to throw some passes with me in the alley before the dinner rush. It was the best he could offer, five minutes in the alley, but that wasn't good enough for me. I walked out, leaving him holding that football."

Marco shook his head and looked at me. He was trying so hard to keep his composure. "That's the last image I have of him, staring after me holding that damn football."

My heart broke as Marco couldn't help but let the tears fall from his eyes. "An hour later my father had a heart attack just as the dinner rush hit. I wasn't there to help him. He died in that kitchen. He died because of me."

Nathan's eyes welled up with tears, too, yet he remained unshaken in his resolve. "My father won't die because of me," Nathan spouted. "He did this to himself. All he had to do was listen."

"Sometimes listening isn't enough," Marco said. "All I had to do was listen, too. My dad needed my help, but I didn't care. He was doing the best he could, but I didn't want to hear it."

"I like you, Marco," Nathan said, wiping his cheek. "I think you're a good guy. I'm sorry about your father, but it's too late for mine."

"That's what I'm trying to tell you," Marco countered in frustration. "It's *not* too late. You don't have to go through with this. Do you know what I wouldn't give right now for five minutes in that alley with my father? I'd do anything to throw that football around with him, to tell him I'm sorry. I would do anything for that chance."

Marco took another step forward. "It's too late for me, Nathan, and that's a heavy burden to bear. I don't get a second chance. But you do."

Nathan stared at Marco for a moment, making me hope he'd gotten the message. But instead, he dropped the knife and pulled his father to his feet, even though Churchill's legs were weak and unsteady, and his eyes could barely open.

Tears spilled down Nathan's cheeks as he said to Marco, "Your father *was* a good man." He backed his dad further over the roof's edge. "That's where our story differs."

Marco inched closer to me, only a few feet away then as he gave his final plea, "Your father might be a bad man, but he doesn't deserve to die."

"You know what the worst part of this is?" Nathan asked as though he hadn't even been listening. He released his grip on Churchill with one hand and pulled out a crumpled, bloody letter, holding it up to his father's face. "In this letter, my father told his employees that no matter who bought the business" -Nathan drew his next words out slowly and let them linger in the cold night air- "he would *always* be New Chapel's Santa Claus." He closed his fist around the letter and threw it at my feet.

At once Marco made a move to grab me but froze when Nathan turned toward him. He was silent for a long moment then said, "Go on. Take your wife. Get her out of here. I don't think either of you should see what happens next."

Without a second's hesitation, Marco lifted me off of the cold, graveled rooftop and carried me away from the edge, untying my hands as Nathan continued his gloomy proclamation to his father.

"You want to be New Chapel's Santa Claus?" he asked, his hands twisting around his father's collar. "You couldn't spend five minutes with me, but you want to be *their* Santa Claus?" Nathan's final words came out even colder than the air around him. "Then they can have you."

"No!" I cried as Nathan gave his father a shove. Churchill's arms windmilled as he fell backward onto the roof's rim, where he hung suspended, his upper body dangling over the side. Marco and I both rushed forward, Marco grabbing Nathan by the coat and dragging him away from the edge. Churchill's Santa hat fell from his head as his neck bent backward over the crowd. I dropped onto the rooftop, grabbing his legs and holding on with all of my weight.

From behind us, the New Chapel police rushed forward. Several officers lifted Churchill from the ledge and back to safety while Reilly and another officer wrestled Nathan to the ground.

As Nathan was taken away, fighting and shouting, and Reilly stayed to wait for the emergency medical team to arrive, Marco sat down against the stairwell wall, his head tipped forward, his hands closed, trembling all over. I slipped off my long red velvet coat, sat down beside him, and wrapped it around him. No words were spoken by either of us, just an outpouring of emotion, long overdue. I put my head on his chest and wept with him.

CHAPTER FIFTEEN

After the police had taken our statements and the medical team had cleared us to leave, and after meeting up with my family and friends to let them know we were safe, Marco and I decided to spend the rest of our Christmas Eve alone at home. Our three-legged mutt, Seedy, had flopped all three of her paws down on the couch cushions behind Marco's head and our rescue cat Smoke lay curled up in my lap.

I rested my head on Marco's chest and let him hold me as an old black-and-white Christmas movie played quietly on the television. We were talking more openly than we ever had, connecting more deeply than I'd ever hoped. We laughed together easily, but it was then I realized that we could cry together as well.

Late into the night Marco finally pulled me from my cozy couch slumber and tucked me into bed. He pulled the covers up, kissed me on the cheek and I heard him say, "Thank you," before I fell into a deeply satisfying sleep.

Christmas morning I woke to the curtains being drawn back, revealing the bright morning sunshine. I could hear Seedy's paws scurrying on the hardwood floor of the bedroom, wanting to jump up beside me, as Smoke made his way onto my pillow and rubbed his wet feline nose against my forehead. "I'm up," I said groggily and then looked at my husband who was already dressed. "I'm up."

"Finally," Marco said. "We're already late."

He wouldn't tell me what we were late for as I hurried to brush my teeth and discard my thick blue robe for a comfy winter outfit. He wouldn't say who the presents were for as he piled them into the back seat of our car. Most importantly though, he wouldn't explain why he had such a big smile as he drove me downtown and parked in front of Bloomers.

My excitement grew as I helped him unload the gifts, wondering what he had planned. But then I noticed that the shop was empty and dark. "Why are we at Bloomers? There's no one here."

"Follow me."

With boxes piled high in my arms, I followed him to Down The Hatch where the door flew open and Jillian ran out to greet us. As excited as a ten-year-old, she took my arm and led me into the bar, with Marco right behind.

I set the wrapped presents down and gazed around the room in astonishment. Lottie and Grace were hanging the last string of holiday lights around the sconces on the walls; Rosa was lighting red and green candles placed in the center of every table; my mom and dad were at the back decorating a small Christmas tree; and cheerful, holiday music played over the speakers.

I didn't know what to say. I turned to find Marco watching me take it all in and asked, "How did you manage all this?"

Lottie answered, "Marco called us first thing this morning, sweetie. We didn't have much time, but judging by that big smile of yours, I think we really pulled it off."

"Abs, I wish you could see the look on your face," Jillian said. "Speaking of which," she licked her thumb and wiped it under one of my eyes, "mascara smudge."

Marco grabbed two glasses of champagne from the tinsel-laden bar as I took turns hugging my mom and dad, Rosa, Grace, and Lottie. "This is incredible," I said, gazing around again.

"That's not all," Mom added. "Marco has invited all of our families to celebrate Christmas here, as well. There's plenty of room for everyone, and now this place is properly decorated."

After the decorations were finalized, we gathered around the tables to discuss the previous night's harrowing events. At a knock on the door, Marco rose to let in Sergeant Reilly. Dressed in his street clothes and a heavy winter jacket, he greeted everyone, took off his jacket, and accepted a glass of champagne. Then he sat down next to me and pulled out a Christmas card.

"Tuck it away and save it for later," he said quietly, his cheeks turning red. "It's for you and Marco."

"Does this mean we're not in trouble, Sarge?" I teased.

"I didn't say that." He cleared his throat and then in his most authoritative tone said, "You clearly don't have any regard for your own safety, Abby, and you continually place yourself in danger. However," he paused, then broke into a slight smile, "I have to say, you do manage to get the job done."

"You know me," I said. "I never back down from a challenge."

"Just be assured that after saving Churchill's life, there won't be any charges filed against you. Honestly, after word gets around, I'm sure you'll be called a hero."

"The florist who saved Christmas," Dad said, smiling at me proudly.

"I like the sound of that," I said, "but I didn't do it alone." I took my husband's hand in mine. "I couldn't have done it without Marco." Then I looked around the room at my friends and family. "Actually, every single person in this room helped us."

"Tell us, Sergeant," Grace said. "How is our dear Santa Claus?"

"Mr. Churchill is still recovering in the hospital. We haven't been told the extent of his injuries, but we do know that he will live."

"And Nathan?" I asked.

"Nathan was treated for minor wounds and taken to jail," Reilly said. "No bond this time, though. He's facing enough charges to keep him locked up for many celebrations to come." Reilly paused to sip some champagne. "He did quite a bit of talking last night, most of it about how he was supposed to inherit Churchill's, although he was hard to understand sometimes. He cried through a lot of it."

"Nathan wanted to run that store," Marco said, shaking his head in sympathy. "I still don't understand why his father wanted to sell the business instead of handing it over to his son."

"Here's what we found out," Reilly said. "When Nathan came home last week for Christmas break, he had to tell his father that he'd flunked out of college. That was when Churchill told him he wouldn't hand over his store to anyone without a business degree. It's unfortunate, but Nathan simply couldn't handle the college courses. So he had to return home knowing he would be a disappointment to his father. And that was when we think he began to fall apart."

"I know how that feels," I said, recalling the terrible depression I'd been in after being booted out of law school. "Did you learn how Nathan found Churchill's letter to his employees?"

"I did," Reilly said. "It seems Nathan dropped his sister off at the store yesterday morning so she could prepare for her elf role. He knew his father would be busy getting ready to play Santa, so he snuck up to Churchill's office to sit at his desk, wanting to know what it would feel like to take over the business. Then he saw the stack of envelopes and looked inside one."

Continuing, Reilly said, "That was when Nathan read his father's letter informing his employees that he planned to retire at the end of the year. He stated that he would sell his business to someone who had the expertise to bring new life to the old building. Apparently, the store hasn't been profitable for a long time. Then Nathan went down to the workshop in a rage to confront his father."

Marco leaned back in his chair and began to piece the story together. "Nathan returns home in shame to tell his dad that he flunked out of college, after which Churchill basically disinherits him by deciding to sell his business. That's a pretty drastic reaction."

"Sometimes drastic is the only choice you have," Lottie argued. "I can relate to what Churchill was going through. Remember, I have four boys myself, so I know that couldn't have been an easy decision."

Rosa spoke up then. "I don't agree. Mr. Churchill is all business, all the time, even on Christmas. I think the decision was an easy one for him."

Marco continued, "Nathan finds the letter and takes it to the workshop to confront his dad. Do you know what happened from there?"

Reilly nodded. "During the ensuing argument, Nathan tried to stop his father from leaving the workshop. Churchill pushed him away and Nathan impaled his hand on an exposed nail when he tried to catch himself. That's where all the blood came from."

"And that," I said, "is exactly when Mrs. Guilford was at the back door of the workshop getting ready to hang her mistletoe."

"How did Nathan get his dad out of the workshop?" Marco asked.

"He didn't," Reilly answered. "Nathan continued to struggle with his dad and got blood all over the Santa suit. Churchill left the workshop on his own to clean up. Nathan forced himself onto the elevator with his father and followed him to the private bathroom on the third floor. That is when Churchill sustained his traumatic injuries."

"What about the blood by that back stairwell?" I asked. "I found a trail of blood leading to the stairwell, but both Nathan and his dad used the elevator."

Reilly answered, "Nathan used the elevator on the way up but not on the way down. After he tied up his dad and left him on the roof, Nathan became paranoid. He said he was afraid someone would see him, so he took the back stairwell from the roof to the first floor and disappeared into the crowd. He must have still been bleeding."

"Was Churchill up on the roof all day?" I asked.

"He was," Reilly answered. "For almost eight hours." He stopped me before I could speak. "Yes, Abby, you were right. The investigation was rushed."

"And I was right about the emergency exit, too," I said. "I don't want to think about what would've happened if that alarm hadn't gone off."

"I still would have found you," Marco said as he placed his arm around me.

"But I wasn't right about everything," I admitted. "I was certain Marcille was somehow involved. Even after I saw her try to stop Nathan's fistfight with the substitute Santa Claus, I still thought she had a hand in Churchill's disappearance."

"I was wrong, too," Rosa announced. "I have always held a grudge against Marcille for taking the manager job from me, but she kept the whole business running smoothly. She even made sure the countdown continued and the star was lit. Churchill made the right decision in hiring her. I still despise what the woman did to me, yet I do have to admire her strength."

"Did you find out why Nathan returned to Churchill's that afternoon?" Marco asked Reilly.

"The detectives believe he went back to get the envelope he'd dropped in the workshop, but I think he had a different plan in mind. I believe Nathan thought the police would shut the whole store down when his father went missing. I think he wanted to sneak his father off of the roof once everyone had left, but when he saw that the store was running as if nothing had happened, he snapped."

"I wonder what will happen to Churchill's now," I said, "and the celebration."

"Churchill isn't the only shop owner on the square," Marco answered. "I'm confident that we won't be alone in making sure the celebration continues for many years to come."

"This was the most widely attended celebration in the town's history," Reilly added. "I don't think it's going anywhere."

With that, my dad held up his glass and we joined him in a toast.

"Well," Reilly said, leaning back in his chair, "I'm glad you were all here today so I could thank you for your help. Even, you, Sergeant Knight." Reilly gave my dad a coy smile. "I knew you were up to something at that police booth. You never talk that much."

"You know I don't like working against the police force," Dad said. "Maybe if you would listen to my daughter next time, I wouldn't have to."

"If there *is* a next time," Reilly said, winking at me, "maybe I will."

Everyone exchanged holiday wishes with Reilly as Marco and I walked him to the door. "Go home and enjoy your family," I said, rising on my tiptoes to hug him.

"I have one more stop before I head home to celebrate," Reilly said as he put on his jacket.

"Speaking of celebrations," I said, "was anyone down on the square even aware of what happened last night?"

"There were only a few interruptions," Reilly replied. "One woman claims she was hit in the face by a falling Santa hat. She came to the station this morning, *Christmas morning*, demanding that I take a statement from her. She's claiming Churchill's is at fault and she wants to sue, said she would be back at the station this afternoon with her lawyer. That's where I'm headed now."

I stopped him. "She didn't happen to have a young boy with her, did she?"

"Yeah, she did," Reilly answered. "A sweet little tyke with big blue eyes."

Ah, Rhondella. "Well, good luck with that," I said. I gave him another hug and wished him a Merry Christmas. Marco shook his hand, and Reilly was off.

We sat back down and continued talking. Soon we were joined by Rosa's mom and son, followed by Jillian's husband and daughter. Eventually, the bar was full of family and happy chatter. My brothers and their families began arriving then, and so did Marco's. And as the carols played in the background, I had to keep reminding myself that this was actually happening. I was having Christmas with my husband.

After everyone had exchanged and opened their gifts my dad pulled me aside. He had one last present sitting in his lap. He waved Marco over to join us by the Christmas tree. "I got this for you," he said to Marco. "I'm sorry for how I acted yesterday. You're a good man, and I'm proud to call you my son."

"You didn't have to get me anything," Marco said.

"Hey," my dad's voice was firm. He handed Marco the present. "You saved my daughter once again. This is the least I could do."

"Honestly, Jeffrey," Marco said. "I think this time Abby saved me."

Marco opened the wrapping and pulled his present from the box. He held the gift in front of him and stared at it, his eyes starting to glisten as he smiled. My dad reached out to shake my husband's hand, so Marco handed me the gift – a brand new leather football.

Marco leaned over and tightened his arms around my dad. "Thank you," he said quietly.

"Why don't you two go out and throw the ball around," Dad suggested and patted the arm of his wheelchair. "I'd go with you but my legs don't work so well. I'm guessing your aim isn't too good either." He gave Marco a wink.

Needing no more encouragement, Marco and I bundled up and headed outside. Downtown New Chapel was peaceful, its streets empty, belying the fateful events of the night before. As we made our way towards the courthouse lawn, snowflakes began to float softly to the ground, sparkling in the winter sunshine.

Marco tossed me the ball, laughing when I missed the pass, then caught my return toss easily, enjoying the game with the merriment of a child. This was what Christmas should always have been for my husband, I thought. This was the joy I'd wanted him to experience with me.

"How did your dad know about the football?" Marco asked, tossing the ball again.

I caught the ball and lifted my shoulders but didn't give him an answer.

"It's a very thoughtful gift," he said, holding the ball in his hands, "but I think I know a little boy who might want this football even more than I do."

I gave Marco a big smile, finally realizing what little Thomas had whispered into Santa's ear, which had caused my husband to tear up. He'd asked for a football, and Marco wanted to fulfill Santa's promise. "I think he would love it."

Marco smiled back at me, his thoughts running in the same direction. "I'll bet you Thomas is with his mom at the police station right now."

"It can't be a coincidence," I agreed. "Not today."

"Do you think your mom will mind if we borrow her costumes one more time?"

"I don't think she'll mind at all," I answered. We walked back to the store hand in hand. I looked up at him with a renewed spirit, no longer worried about our future, but looking forward to it instead. "Merry Christmas, Marco," I finally said.

And for the very first time, he responded, "Merry Christmas, Sunshine."

ACKNOWLEDGMENTS

First I'd like to thank my son, Jason, for all his hard work and talent in helping create this delightful, moving tale of the ability of love and determination to move mountains.

I'd also like to thank my daughter, Julia, for continuing to be the inspiration for my courageous heroine, Abby Knight, a young woman who never backs down from a challenge.

And last, here's to all the Scrooges out there who may have hidden reasons for their "Bah, humbug," attitudes.

Merry Christmas.

Flower Shop Mystery Series

MUM'S THE WORD
SLAY IT WITH FLOWERS
DEARLY DEPOTTED
SNIPPED IN THE BUD
ACTS OF VIOLETS
A ROSE FROM THE DEAD
SHOOTS TO KILL
EVIL IN CARNATIONS
SLEEPING WITH ANEMONE
DIRTY ROTTEN TENDRILS
NIGHT OF THE LIVING DANDELION
TO CATCH A LEAF
NIGHTSHADE ON ELM STREET
SEED NO EVIL
THROW IN THE TROWEL
A ROOT AWAKENING
FLORIST GRUMP
MOSS HYSTERIA
YEWS WITH CAUTION
TULIPS TOO LATE – Spring Novella
A FROND IN NEED – Summer Novella

Goddess of Greene St. Mysteries

STATUE OF LIMITATIONS
A BIG FAT GREEK MURDER

Continue reading for chapter one –
A BIG FAT GREEK MURDER
The Goddess of Greene St. Mysteries

A BIG FAT GREEK MURDER

GODDESS OF GREENE ST. MYSTERIES

KATE COLLINS

It's All Greek To ME
by Goddess Anon

This has to be a fast post because I'm due at a rehearsal dinner in an hour, and I have yet to change. Lucky me, you say? Sounds like a good time? "Humbug" is my reply. Getting all dolled up after a day of work so I can spend my evening pretending to be overjoyed for a happy couple is not my idea of a good time. Lest ye forget, I was once one-half of a so-called "happy couple."

It won't be easy for me to watch the soon-to-be-wed duo entwine arms, sip champagne, and promise to be loyal to each other forever because I know that forever is a long, long time.

I realize it seems I've soured on marriage, but I haven't completely given up. I keep hoping to find my Prince Charming out there somewhere. But who knows where that will be? Surely not here in my small Michigan hometown. I can't even find a decent white wine, let alone a white knight—unless my luck is changing. I don't believe in miracles, but there does seem to be a certain magic in the air lately. Who knows? Maybe it could happen tonight.

Look at the time, and I still don't have a clue as to what I should wear. How does one attract a white knight? Black, perhaps?

Till tomorrow, this is Goddess Anon bidding you adío.

P.S. That's Greek for good-bye. Wish me luck!

CHAPTER ONE

Friday

I posted the blog, closed my laptop, and turned in my chair to look at the small bedroom closet overflowing with clothes from my former life. Somewhere in that mess was the dress I'd be wearing to the rehearsal dinner. A white knight. *Hmm.* Dark wavy hair, strong jaw, soulful eyes that seem to look through me, melt me like butter . . . and there was Case Donnelly once again creep- ing into my thoughts. After inviting him to meet me for a drink after the rehearsal dinner, and his nonchalant ex- cuse, I cursed myself for taking the chance. A white knight was out there somewhere for me, but clearly it wasn't Case Donnelly.

I took a deep breath and began the hunt for my black dress.

Fifteen minutes later, after one last look in the bath- room mirror, I kissed my ten-year-old son, Nicholas, good-bye, blew a kiss at my youngest sister, Delphi, who'd stayed home to babysit, grabbed my purse and a light- weight coat, and hurried out to my white SUV for the ten- minute ride to the Parthenon, my grandparents' diner.

My phone rang through the car's speakers, and I tapped a button to answer, "Hello."

"Thenie, it's Dad. I need your help."

"I'm almost at the Parthenon, Pops. What's up?"

"Mrs. Bird is out back pecking at the new rose bushes and demanding to see you, Delphi is babysitting your son, and I've got a line of customers out the door. I know you promised your mother that you'd help out at the diner, but I could really use your help."

"Might I mention again that we need seasonal employees?"

"You can lecture me when you get here."

"I can't make it right now, Pops. I'll call Delphi. She can bring Nicholas with her."

"Thanks, but we need a landscape consultant or we're going to lose Mrs. Bird's business."

"Let Delphi ring up the customers. You can handle Mrs. Bird."

"That's not the answer I was looking for."

"I'll be there as soon as I can, Pops."

Landscape consultant was on the opposite end of the spectrum from my former job as a newspaper reporter in Chicago. The vibrant tourist town of Sequoia was equally distant on the spectrum from the bustling Windy City that my son and I used to call home. The two cities shared the same water, but the breeze blowing east from Lake Michigan felt different. It smelled different, fresher perhaps.

If circumstances hadn't forced me to move back into the big family home, I'd still be running around the city, interviewing people and sitting at a computer until late at night to turn in my "noteworthy" articles. Instead, I was able to be outdoors working with plants and flowers and the cheerful people who came to our garden center to buy them. And at last, after one month of working in the office, learning the ins and outs of the business end of the operation, my dad felt I was ready to try my hand at land- scape design. Turned out, I loved it.

I parked my car in the public lot on the block behind Greene Street and scurried up the alley. I entered through a back gate in the high fence and made my way to the outdoor eating area. With white wrought-iron tables and chairs, a concrete patio floor painted Grecian blue, white Greek-style columns on each corner, and blue-and-white lights strung around the entire perimeter, Yiayiá and Pappoús could not have made it look cozier or more inviting.

At least I thought so. But the guests didn't seem to be enjoying it. In fact, there was a distinctly unhappy *vibe* in the air, as Delphi would say. My mother was standing in front of the kitchen door, worrying the thick gold Greek bracelet she was never without.

As I approached, my feet already hurting, Mama said, "It's not good, Athena. The groom-to-be hasn't shown up, and no one can reach him. What are you wearing?"

My mother had on black slacks with a Grecian blue blouse, or, as Mama referred to blue, "the color of the Ionian Sea." Unfortunately, I hadn't gotten the memo, so I was the oddball in my short black dress and strappy black heels. And no prince in sight.

"I didn't know there was a dress code." I glanced around at the tables, full of worried, whispering guests. "Maybe he got cold feet. Did he show up for the rehearsal?"

"They're having the wedding rehearsal after the dinner because some of the family members had to work."

"Why such a big crowd for a rehearsal dinner?" I asked. "Usually it's just for the wedding party."

"The Blacks decided to include the families of the wedding party," Mama said. "They're wealthy, and they pay very well. I wasn't about to question them on their decision."

I scanned the area, making mental notes. The wedding party was gathered at the head table, where Mandy, the bride-to-be, in a yellow silk dress, was being consoled not only by her bridesmaids, but also her parents and my oldest sister, Selene. Mitchell, the bride's twin brother and best man, stood directly behind them, checking his watch and looking perturbed, while maid of honor Tonya stood off to the side, talking quietly on her phone.

"What about the groom's parents?" I asked. "Have they heard from him?"

"His parents aren't here," Mama said. "Apparently, they declined the invitation."

My sister Maia joined us, breathless with news. "I just heard that two of Brady's groomsmen have gone to his apartment to see what the holdup is. He lives down the road, so it shouldn't take long—and aren't those my heels, Athena? And why are you so dressed up?"

Mama licked her thumb to wipe away a smudge from under Maia's eye, causing my sister to roll her head to the side.

"Never mind about her outfit," Mama said, "and good for those brave boys. Yiayiá and Pappoús will be pleased. You know how upset they get if their food gets cold. Hold *still*, Maia."

That was so typical of our Greek family—more concerned about the guests missing a meal than the bride-to-be missing her groom.

Submitting to my mother's ministrations, Maia rolled her eyes, while I tried to hide my smile with a cough.

Maia was born after me; we were the two middle sisters of four, all named after Greek goddesses—Selene after the moon goddess, me after Athena, goddess of war and wisdom, and Maia after goddess of the fields. The exception was our youngest sister, Delphi, who was named in honor of the Oracle of Delphi. Stymied that she wasn't a "goddess," Delphi had long ago decided that she had the gift of foresight and was a true modern-day oracle. The remarkable thing was that sometimes she got her predictions right.

Also remarkable was how much Maia, Selene, and Delphi looked like our mother, shortish in stature, with fuller curves, lots of curly black hair, and typical Greek features. I, on the other hand, took after my father's English side of the family, inheriting his light brown hair, slender body, oval face, and softer features. In family photos, I was the gawky, pale-skinned girl in the back row standing beside the tall, pale-skinned man.

Selene broke away from the inconsolable bride and headed in our direction, an exasperated look on her face—coincidentally, the same expression Mama was wearing. Because she was also part of the wedding party, Selene wore a black-and-white sheath dress and heels instead of the waitress outfit.

"Selene," Mama said, "go back and ask the bride's mother whether we should serve the appetizers now. These poor people have to eat something."

"I just came from there," Selene replied, looking even more exasperated than before. "I don't think they're in any mood to—"

Mama gave her "the look," and Selene did an about-face, slipping away obediently.

My grandmother joined our little group then, asking if she and Pappoús should start serving the lemon rice soup known as *avgolemono* (pronounced "ahv-lemono").

"No, Yiayiá," I said. "We're waiting for the groom to arrive."

"Still?" she asked in her high, raspy voice. "But the people need food."

Maia looked at me, trying to suppress another eye roll. I couldn't help but laugh, rubbing my grandmother's back to calm her down.

"Why you laugh?" Yiayiá asked with a scowl. Standing at a mere five feet high, she wore a black blouse, a long, full, black-print cotton skirt, and thick-soled black shoes. The only brightness in her outfit was a blue— excuse me—Ionian Sea–colored scarf that wrapped around her white hair, wound into its usual tight knot at the back of her head.

"It shouldn't be long, Mama," my mother said to her, shooting us a glare. "We expect them at any moment."

"*Endáksi,*" she said with a sigh and a shrug. *Okay.* Wearing her usual world-weary expression, she headed back into the kitchen to share the news with Pappoús.

Suddenly, the two absent groomsmen came jogging around the corner of the restaurant, out of breath and wild-eyed. "Brady," one gasped, holding his side, "he's been hurt. Badly."

"Taken," the second groomsmen said, bending over to gulp air, "to the hospital."

As the guests rose to their feet in concern, the bride gathered her full skirt and ran toward the two men, grabbing onto the shirt front of one. "Trevor, is Brady dead?"

In between gulps of air, Trevor replied, "He was—unconscious—when the paramedics—took him away."

Mandy took a step backward as though she'd been pushed. "Then he's alive?"

"We don't know," Patrick, the other groomsman said, "We found him on his apartment floor with a pair of—"

"Patrick," Trevor snapped, giving a subtle nod in Mandy's direction.

"With a pair of what?" Mandy cried, grabbing his shirt front again. "Tell me. With *what*?"

Trevor's chin began to tremble, and a tear ran down his cheek. "Scissors in his back."

There was a collective gasp. My mother made the sign of the cross. Maia's mouth dropped open. Selene froze in place. I spotted Tonya, the bridesmaid who'd been on the cell phone, turn to give the other bridesmaids a knowing look, and I instantly filed it away.

"The police are on their way, Mandy," Patrick said. "They'll be able to tell you more."

The bride-to-be collapsed in a puddle of yellow silk, sobbing hysterically, "Brady's dead. I know he's dead. What will I do? Oh my God, what will I do?"

Her parents helped her to her chair and sat on either side of her, rubbing her hands, while her brother strode toward the two groomsmen to have a whispered conference. My mother hurried over to talk to the bride's mother, who was consoling her distraught daughter. That was when I spotted Selene, her face ashen, slip around the guests and disappear into the kitchen.

Before I could follow her, Mama returned to say quietly to us, "I just spoke with Mandy and her parents. They're going to stay here until the police arrive. Maia, go tell Yiayiá and Pappoús we'll start serving the soup afterward."

"Maia, wait!" I called, as she started toward the kitchen. "Mama, no one is going to stay for dinner. This is supposed to be a celebration."

"But they must eat!" she cried. "Think of all the food waiting for them."

"Athena is right, Mama," Maia said. "They've just had horrible news. They're not going to sit down and dine now."

Mama put her hand over her forehead. "Then go tell your grandparents that, Maia."

"I'll tell them," I said, and headed inside to deliver the message and find out why Selene had slipped away.

"Yiayiá, Pappoús, the dinner has been canceled," I announced. "The groom was taken to the hospital with a serious injury."

Pappoús stopped stirring the soup, and Yiayiá straightened, putting one hand on her lower back. Almost in unison they said, "But the people have to eat!"

"It's not appropriate to serve food when there's been a calamity," I explained.

"Calamity is right," Yiayiá said grumpily, eyeing all the food.

"The groom is injured, sure," Pappoús said in his thick Greek accent, "but what about the others?"

"They'll be going home soon." I glanced around but didn't see my sister. "Yiayiá, did you see Selene come through the kitchen?"

"She's sitting out there by herself," Yiayiá replied, nodding her head toward the swinging doors to the diner. "Maybe you can talk to her. She won't tell me what's wrong."

I found my sister in a booth in the empty diner, staring blankly into space. She had scooted to the far end, with her back to the wall and her feet hanging off the edge. I slid in opposite her and reached for her hand.

"What's wrong, Selene? You look like you just lost your best friend."

Her gaze shifted to mine, and I saw fear in her eyes. Just as she was about to speak, my mother stepped into the room and clapped her hands. "Girls, the police are here. They want everyone outside except for Yiayiá and Pappoús. *Páme!*"

As soon as Mama left, Selene bent her head and sobbed. I hadn't seen my oldest sister cry since we were children, and it startled me. Selene had always been strong and bold, the fearless firstborn, a role model for her sisters. Now she wept as though her heart was broken.

"Selene, what is it?"

"Stay with me, Athena," she sobbed, reaching for my hand. "Don't leave my side."

"I won't, but tell me why."

"The scissors in Brady's back? I think they're mine."

About The Author

Kate Collins is the author of the best-selling Flower Shop Mystery series. Her books have made the New York Times Bestseller list, the Barnes & Noble mass market mystery best-sellers' lists, the Independent Booksellers' best-seller's lists, as well as booksellers' lists in the U.K. and Australia. The first three books in the FSM series are now available on audiobook. Kate's new series, GODDESS OF GREENE ST. MYSTERIES, arrived in 2019. STATUE OF LIMITATIONS is the first book in the series, with the second book, A BIG FAT GREEK MURDER, available December 2020, and a third book in the works.

In January of 2016, Hallmark Movies & Mysteries channel aired the first Flower Shop Mystery series movie, MUM'S THE WORD, followed by SLAY IT WITH FLOWERS and DEARLY DEPOTTED. The movies star Brooke Shields, Brennan Elliott, Beau Bridges and Kate Drummond.

Kate started her career writing children's stories for magazines and eventually published historical romantic suspense novels under the pen name Linda Eberhardt and Linda O'Brien. Seven romance novels later, she switched to her true love, mysteries.

Printed in Great Britain
by Amazon

32262126R10088